DEATH IS A FAST HORSE

Gunfire boomed on the pastoral air of the setting. Frank wondered who the hell was firing at him, and why.

Then two more rifle shots cracked through the sweet morning air, and Frank was startled when he saw a red mare and a rider laid flat against the saddle suddenly charging out from behind a boulder.

The horse broke into a fast gallop. It rode straight at Frank, the metal shoes of its hooves flashing in the sunlight.

Frank barely had time to roll away from the course of the charging animal before being kicked by the flashing hooves . . .

Special Preview!

*Turn to the back of this book
for a sneak-peek excerpt
of the new epic western series . . .*

THE HORSEMEN

. . . the sprawling, unforgettable story of a family of horse breeders and trainers—from the Civil War South to the Wild West.

BROTHERS IN BLOOD

COLD DEATH

DANIEL ST. JAMES

BERKLEY BOOKS, NEW YORK

BROTHERS IN BLOOD: COLD DEATH

A Berkley Book / published by arrangement with
the author

PRINTING HISTORY
Berkley edition / June 1992

ISBN: 0-425-13302-8

A BERKLEY BOOK ® TM 757, 375
Berkley Books are published by The Berkley Publishing Group,
200 Madison Avenue, New York, New York 10016.
The name "BERKLEY" and the "B" logo
are trademarks belonging to Berkley Publishing Corporation.

PRINTED IN THE UNITED STATES OF AMERICA

10 9 8 7 6 5 4 3 2 1

COLD DEATH

prologue

FEBRUARY

BY MIDNIGHT, THE SNOWSTORM HAD BECOME A genuine blizzard.

Most of the residents of Kelly Bay were snug in their beds, happy to content themselves with dreams of green summer and the warm blue waters of the bay. Karl Swenson was an exception.

Up until twenty minutes ago, he'd been sleeping, or trying to anyway, lying awake in the bed where he'd first made love to his wife eight years ago. She still slept next to him, a little heavier now, her long dark hair streaked with gray, but still the same tender, bright, pretty woman he'd taken for his bride.

He reached over in the darkness and touched her hip gently. She responded by moaning dreamily in her sleep.

There in the shadows of their bedroom, the wind crying like a dying animal, he dressed. He was careful to dress lightly: a pair of trousers, a pair of socks but no shoes, and a shirt with no collar. To anyone who knew the man, his attire was curious. One of the leading citizens of Kelly Bay, he was something of a dude. People often smiled, most without a certain affection, at the way he got all peacocked up just to go to work on a sunny morning.

1

He took a last look at his wife, bowed his head a moment, and then left the room.

He went down the hallway, not having to tip-toe because the wind was so loud, to the large square room where his two young daughters slept.

They always left their door open so that if they had particularly bad nightmares, they could come scurrying in to Daddy's protective arms.

He peeked in, saw that they were deeply asleep, and crept over to their bed. Each girl—one six years old, the other five—got a tender kiss on her damp little forehead.

He hesitated a moment, staring down at both of them.

In the long run, they would be better off, he thought. In the long run, they would survive what he was about to do.

He clenched his fists, not wanting to give in to the tears that had started filling his eyes, and he left their room.

Three minutes later, Karl Swenson opened the back door of his fine, white two-story house and walked straight to the shed where he kept two buggies and a horse. His family loved going for rides. The wind almost knocked him to the ground. He had to slant his body into the wind to make any kind of progress at all. And his feet, without shoes, became numb almost immediately.

Maybe this is what hell would be like. Not flames and vile men with comic pitchforks, but just endless bitter howling night, like the surface of some alien planet, just the endless cry of the elements and total isolation for Karl himself.

It took five minutes to reach the shed, then things went quickly. He found the kerosene can in the corner. It had plenty of fuel.

He went over and ran a hand over the rump of the sleeping bay mare his daughters liked so well. He always

felt sorry for her on nights like this. He understood why
the girls wanted the horse to sleep inside the house with
the rest of the family.

Then he grabbed the can and went back outside. He
walked around to the downwind side of the shed.

He had considered doing it inside the shed, but he was
afraid that the fire would spread to the hay, and that the
mare would be killed.

He did it then, poured the kerosene all over himself
and set a match to his fuel-soaked trousers. His scream
was nearly as loud as the wind. At first, but then the
flames began to flap and play higher and higher, brilliant
yellow against the dark night and the flecking snow, and
he just crumpled to the ground, too delirious to cry out any
longer.

And as he had so long hoped, as he had so long planned,
Karl Swenson, a most successful man in Kelly Bay, was
dead.

After a time, the wind ate the flames and robbed the
night of the warm yellow flapping fire, and there was just
darkness and the crying wind.

His wife found him in the morning.

chapter
one

APRIL
Tuesday

BACK IN LONDON, THERE WERE ALREADY OPER-
ettas about the Royal Canadian Mounted Police. Beefy
actors in the familiar red jackets, blue trousers, and high
boots of the Mounties trod the stage, much to the delight
of young English girls who swooned each time one of the
redcoats sang a ballad.

In the Canadian provinces, things were slightly different. So far this year, the men in the red coats had not
sung a single ballad, but various members had been shot,
stabbed, drowned, or killed by the occasional case of cholera. Some had been lost in bitter blizzards, poisoned by
tainted meat served in the barracks, stomped by moose,
beset by gunrunners, beset by the last straggling crazies
among the last straggling Indian tribes, and ordered by
their superiors not to get married, said superiors believing
that missing your bride could only dull the senses (and
therefore, competence) of the average Mountie.

In other words, things were pretty much as they always
were with that force of red-coated men that brought law
and most times order to the untamed Canadian frontier—
rough, lonely, and frequently dangerous.

4

Those beefy baritones in the London operettas didn't know how lucky they were.

Sergeant David Adams would never get over the sheer raw beauty of the Canadian frontier.

Early this morning he had put his canoe into the deep blue waters of the Cree River and taken himself twenty miles downstream to Kelly Bay. The shore had revealed everything from Indian encampments to small, patched-together mining camps to a glimpse of a Canadian Pacific Railroad trunk line carrying a hurtling train into the soft, sunny afternoon. A family of wolves had run along a half-mile line of shore, friendly and interested in his passage.

Now, as he got out of his canoe and stepped up to the muddy shore, he felt a powerful appetite rumbling through his stomach. He looked forward to a good meal, a good pipe, perhaps a pint of ale, and then a good bed.

Once he was finished with his canoe, he set off for the town itself, which was a quarter of a mile away through a shallow forest of spruce and pine.

Six years ago, Kelly Bay, then little more than a few shacks and a one-room hospital used by area settlers and run by a lone Maryknoll nun, had become the site of a furious if short-lived gold strike. A local Cree had discovered a vein of gold in some nearby hills. There were plenty of white traders around who were eager to cheat him out of his discovery, and white traders being what they are, that's just what they did. For his discovery, the Cree got two good meals, a gut full of raw rumrunner whiskey, and the promise of a white whore. As it happened, the Cree proved to be an angry drunk, and the white whore begged off, afraid.

The traders inflicted themselves on Kelly Bay for the next fourteen months.

Almost at once, the small town tripled, then quadrupled, in population. Suddenly there was a main street with two dozen false fronts; there were tents, shacks and soddies for the miners to sleep in.

One day a paddlewheeler came up the Cree and let loose more than seven hundred new miners, most wearing red shirts and crazed gleams in their eyes. Most were white, though maybe fifty were black, and they spoke so many languages the air was filled with an ear-jarring cacophony.

They stayed two years in all and attracted whores, thieves, confidence men, and parasites of every kind. In one day there were six murders and eight hangings. Violent racial clashes broke out—one black man was castrated, one white man had both his eyes dug out with a Bowie knife. All this was pretty typical for a gold strike. Things always got crazy.

Then somebody noticed that despite the early promise of the strikes, the veins petered out pretty quickly. Indeed, six months had gone by with no major discoveries of precious metals at all.

In the autumn of that year, another paddlewheeler came up the Cree. This time, instead of disgorging miners, it picked them up.

Farther up the Cree, it was said, were gold strikes wondrous to behold. So the miners took their packs, pickaxes, spades, and pans and boarded the paddlewheeler heading due north up the Cree, where surely they would make their fortunes this time.

After the dust settled—plain old dust, alas; not gold dust—Kelly Bay still found itself a pretty big place, one that had become quite prosperous serving not only miners but all the farmers and fur traders and trappers who lived and worked in the area.

The one-room hospital was now a six-room hospital, and there was a regular telegraph station. The train ran just to the west of the town, and on Saturday night, while the good folks stayed home and got ready for Sunday church or mass, the streets were as lewd and bright as any to be found in Dawson or Skagway.

Kelly Bay had become a real town.

Adams found the Swenson house on the south edge of town, a tidy, impressive two-story red brick home sitting on two acres of buffalo grass just now turning from brown to spring green. A black iron fence surrounded a good portion of the yard. Two young girls, bundled up as if it were still winter, threw an orange ball back and forth.

The end of the day was here, shadows growing deep and long, the temperature beginning to drop, white smoke curling up from the brick chimney.

When the girls saw the red-coated man come through the gate, they stopped throwing the ball and watched him carefully. They were silent.

"Hello, girls, is your mother home?"

The two girls looked at each other, as if to make sure that responding to this man was the proper thing to do.

"Mommy!" one of the girls yelled suddenly.

And then she was in the door, just as slight and pretty as he remembered her, the added years only giving her Swedish beauty dignity. Even from here, Adams could see the sorrow in her blue eyes.

When she saw who he was, she opened the door and came running down the walk, straight into his arms.

He held her very tight, recalling briefly how before she'd been Karl's woman, she'd been his.

"It's so good to see you, David," she said, breaking their embrace. By now, her two daughters had gathered around her, tugging on the length of her blue dress and white apron, clinging shyly to her so they could risk a longer glimpse at the stranger.

"Are you hungry?"

Adams smiled. "I could lie and say no."

"We're having pot roast. How does that sound?"

"Do I really need to tell you?"

With that, Anna eased her arm through his and escorted him up the walk to the front door, the girls still clutching her dress.

chapter
two

KELLY BAY HAD FOUR WHOREHOUSES, THREE OF them for workingmen, trappers, traders, and drifters. The women were about what you'd expect, never quite as clean as you'd like, given to the same sloppy drunken behavior as the johns themselves, and not all of them with teeth. And some of them with teeth might have been better off otherwise, given the stench.

There was a fourth whorehouse, this located three-quarters of a mile out of town, a log-cabin version of a mansion with three stories filled with small rooms that gave the place the feeling of a dormitory. Each whore had her own room and was expected to keep it clean and clean-smelling, just as she was expected to keep herself clean and clean-smelling. The madame was a past master on the subject of douching etiquette.

The madame's name was Myra Livermore, and she claimed to be Australian, though the buzz in town was that she was a white woman who'd been abducted by Apaches as a young girl and forced into life as a tribe whore.

Whatever her background, Myra Livermore had made more money here in eleven months than her competitors had in four years, and the reason was simple enough: she catered to what passed for the carriage trade here in Kelly Bay.

Doctors, lawyers, merchants, and even the occasional clergyman (Myra loved to tell the story about the size of this Presbyterian minister she'd once serviced) had sexual urges, too. And so she took care of them.

Downstairs were comfortable furnishings, a player piano, a one-eyed mulatto bouncer who brooked no nonsense from anybody, and good whiskey brought from Montreal.

Upstairs were the rooms the girls took pains to keep clean, a Rochester lamp in every room, fresh bedclothes, and a back entrance in case the local law suddenly bowed to political pressure and came a'raiding some night. The back stairs were a quick way out for all those respectable gents who had reputations to think of.

Then there was the attic.

The entrance was all the way down the third-floor hallway, past all those small, private rooms where you heard giggles and moans and the occasional slap of paid-for sexual violence, and then you came to a locked door.

Myra Livermore controlled who went into the attic and when; only Myra.

As Sergeant David Adams was enjoying his dinner with Anna Swenson and her daughters, Myra Livermore was leading a man into her first-floor office. Once inside, she nodded for him to close the door behind him, and then to have a seat in the plump chair of real leather Myra had put in here to complement the real leather couch, the roll-top desks, and the two four-drawer filing cabinets, all of which proclaimed that Myra Livermore was not just one more seedy madame but was instead a frontier businesswoman of the most enlightened kind.

The library lamp hanging from the ceiling lent the well-appointed room a coziness now that darkness was falling.

The man was dressed all in black, as befitted his occupation, which was mortician. She glanced at his long, almost effeminate fingers and thought how they spent all day probing corpses, draining blood and other fluids to run down into the gutters of his work table. She shuddered, glad that she would never have to let those fingers touch any part of her body.

There were those in Kelly Bay who snickered that this man was a queer, but she knew better. She knew what he really wanted.

Now, fidgeting, he pushed his hand inside his black suitcoat. Moments later, his hand returned to her sight, his fingers fanned a half-dozen greenbacks as if they were props in a magic trick.

"You said you were gonna have to be raisin' your prices, ma'am."

She smiled at the sight of the money. "Looks like you were a good boy and brought plenty."

"You know what I want, ma'am."

She nodded.

"I want to go up to the attic again, ma'am."

"You have to be patient. I have to get things ready."

He had started fidgeting again, obviously afraid that she wasn't going to let him up there tonight.

"You're gonna let me, ain't you, ma'am?"

"You just keep calm, Richard."

"It's all I thought about since last time, ma'am. Goin' back up to the attic." He dropped his eyes, ashamed. "I even have dreams about the attic, ma'am. I can't help myself."

"You'll have to give me a little while."

She got up, a plump woman who nonetheless managed to move with surprising ease.

His fingers shot out and touched her wrist.

As if burned, she jerked her hand away. She tried not to think of all the things those bony fingers had touched.

"I didn't mean nothin' by that, ma'am."

"Never touch me again. Do you understand me?"

He nodded, miserable. It was obvious he was afraid she was going to punish him by not letting him go up to the attic later.

"Now you wait here, Richard." She looked at her wrist as if for some sign of scab or burn. For touching her, he was going to have to pay more than she'd even planned on charging him.

God, why did he have to touch her?

"It's all I think of, ma'am," he said, raising his eyes to the ceiling. "It's all I think of."

Myra went off to get things ready in the attic.

chapter
three

A HEADACHE HAD SENT LIZ CONWAY TO BED early. As a widow and as the sole person to work the surrounding fifty acres, Liz was often tired early in the night.

She undressed in the moonlight falling silver through the cabin window. She and her husband had never had much money to spend, and the cabin was proof of this—a crude, one-room affair not much different from the sod huts the pioneers had built decades earlier. Liz had tried hard to give the room a feminine, homey touch but with such a place, one could only do so much.

Chilled now, she decided to sleep in her shirt. She crawled beneath the covers, her body shivering and covered with goosebumps. She wanted warmth and the peace of sleep, and she hoped she could get to sleep soon.

She huddled under the covers, tucking her hands and wrists between her folded knees and closed her eyes.

Immediately, thoughts of Karl Swenson filled her mind. She was a respectable woman. She should never have had an affair with him. And she should never have been foolish enough to fall in love with him.

She pushed Karl from her mind and thought of her husband. At least she had never betrayed him. Karl hadn't

started coming around until well after her husband was
dead.

Her husband had been steady, reliable, good. Karl had
been handsome, dashing, capable of—

Ah but that wasn't so.

Much as she tried to paint Karl Swenson as evil, she
knew better. He'd simply been a troubled man who had a
problem with drinking.

She squeezed her eyes closed even tighter. She needed
sleep. She began to pray. Oh Lord, grant me peace and
forgive me for breaking your law of adultery. I did not
mean to hurt Mrs. Swenson and the Swenson children.
Please forgive me, Lord. I am not a bad woman.

And then, at last, she fell asleep.

Myra had given Gatineau very specific instructions.

Ride to the west of Liz Conway's cabin, then come down
the rocky hill to the rear of the place. Look in the back
window, and make sure all the lights are out and that she's
sleeping, then sneak around to the front, pull your kerchief
over your face, and go in the front door.

Gatineau followed the moonlit trail, just as Myra had told
him. He dismounted and hid his horse behind the copse of
hardwoods, just as Myra had told him. Then he snuck down
the hill and peered in the rear window of the cabin.

It took two long minutes for his eyes to adjust to the
shadows inside.

He saw pots and pans on the makeshift wooden sink.
He saw newly washed clothes hanging on a line stretching from one corner of the cabin to another. Then he
saw the bed and the woman sleeping in it. He'd seen
Liz Conway around town. She was a true beauty. Even
in sleep, her dark hair and graceful features were pretty
to see.

Even in sleep, she inspired in Gatineau an almost weary lust. He'd been too long without a woman, which was pretty funny when you stopped to think of it, Myra owning a cathouse and everything.

He drew his .44. He hunched low and started to sneak around the side of the cabin.

Liz was a light sleeper. Her husband had taught her to keep his Colt right next to the bed, so as she heard somebody ease open the cabin door she came up from sleep with her gun in her hand.

But she was too late. The shaggy silhouette in the doorway fired two blinding orange-white shots just above her head.

"Throw down your gun or the next one's for you."

Liz was no fool. She did just as the man told her.

"Light a lantern," the man snapped.

She had no choice. She got out of bed, terrified, forgetting for the moment that she wore only a shirt, one that didn't hang far enough to cover the thatch of dark hair at the top of her legs.

When she finally got a kerosene lamp going, she saw that the man was looking at her greedily.

"You've come to the wrong place," she said. "I don't have anything."

He kept his eyes on her sex. "You've got a lot, lady."

But then, as if somebody invisible had slapped him and told him to get back to work, the man started his search. He threw things around. He overturned things. It was obvious that he hadn't found what he was looking for.

He grabbed Liz and slammed her up against the wall. Then he grasped the front of her shirt and ripped it all the way down, till she stood virtually naked in front of him.

He looked as if he were mightily tempted to rape her. He licked his dry lips.

Then, as if again forcing himself to remember why he came here, he slapped her across the face and said, "Where is it?"

"Where is what?"

"You bitch—you know what I'm talking about."

He had to be careful. Myra had told him not to hurt the woman, and she'd also told him not to tell the woman what he was searching for.

"No, I don't have any idea what you're talking about. I really don't."

She couldn't help the tears that came suddenly, the tears she'd been wanting to cry since the night Karl Swenson had doused himself with kerosene and—

The man seemed to be crazed then. He started searching the room again, but this time he kicked and smashed and punched everything in sight, until the one-room cabin was little more than a junk pile. She wondered if it would ever again look like anything civilized.

Now she was colder than ever as he came back to her and started backhanding her across the face.

Hot, salty blood filled her mouth. Her tears became wrenching sobs.

"You bitch. You don't know how bad I want to kill you," he said.

And then he was gone, just as quickly and mysteriously as he'd appeared, smashing his way through the debris-littered floor and stomping out into the night.

For a long time, she lay on the bed, sobbing.

Sleep did not come till she heard a rooster crow.

chapter
four

JUST AS U.S. MARSHAL FRANK ADAMS WAS ABOUT
to set down his schooner of beer and face the man who'd just
called him a name, the man decided to up the ante. He wasn't
going to settle for just a good old all-American fistfight; he
was going to insist on gunplay.

The man's hand was already dropping to his holster.
Frank turned a few inches to his right and then splashed
his beer over the man's face. The man let out a yelp.

Temporarily blinded—and profoundly enraged—the
man's hand couldn't seem to find the gun. Frank took
advantage of this situation by punching the man directly
in the face.

The first time felt so good, he just had to do it a second
time. And then a third.

And considering how much the man had been bothering
him the past half hour—Frank had just stopped in here for
a relaxing shell of beer or two, having spent the last day
and a half riding up from Montana—Frank decided to vent
his anger one more time. He hit the man so hard in the
solar plexus, the man went skittering backwards, eventually
slamming into a card table and chairs that four local thugs
had been smart enough to evacuate earlier.

Frank was just standing there congratulating himself on
a job well done when he saw several of the local thugs start

17

to smile. Before Frank had time to figure out what the grins were all about, he heard the unmistakable sound of a rifle hammer being cocked. He felt the rifle barrel being jammed against the back of his head.

"Shit," Frank muttered to himself.

But life was like that sometimes. You stood in dung up to your neck, and then somebody threw a bucket of puke at you.

"You take that gun of yours out and drop it on the floor," the bartender said.

He spoke with a slight lisp so he was easy enough to identify.

"What if I don't want to?"

"Then I empty this rifle into your head."

"You do that, and you'll be facing a rope."

"I'm willing to take the chance, stranger. Now drop that gun."

Given the odds, and given the determination of the lisping man, Frank eased his hand down to the butt of his revolver, picked it up carefully, then set it on the bar.

Several feet away, the man he'd just beaten was struggling to his feet.

"You shouldn't have ought to done that, mister," the bartender said.

"I shouldn't have ought to done what?" Frank said.

"You shouldn't have ought to beat up my brother that way."

"Then he shouldn't have ought to have been calling me names all night."

"T'weren't his fault."

"Oh, no?"

"He was drunk."

"The poor dear."

"You just watch your mouth, mister."

Now, the drunken man was on his feet again and staggering towards Frank.

The tavern was a single, oblong room with a sod floor and a long slab of wood set on barrels for a bar. There was an outhouse on the hill out back, but many of the men just pissed in one of the shadowy corners of the tavern, which didn't exactly give the place a pleasant aroma.

Frank was just glad he didn't have to eat in here.

The drunken man hit Frank with a decent left hook. Not great, but decent. Frank tasted blood. The sonofabitch. Frank didn't like tasting blood. The next punch landed in Frank's stomach. A lot of people had been kidding Frank lately about his thickening girth, and he now saw why. The punch, which had come in crooked and without a lot of force, hurt more than it should have.

Right then and there, Frank took a pledge to give up beer, cake, and potatoes. Maybe not exactly right away, but soon. Very soon.

When the guy, cheered on by all his greasy thug friends, tried to kick him in the balls, Frank decided to put this guy away for good. He ducked under the barrel of the gun and shot an elbow into the chest of the lisping bartender. The rifle misfired, echoing and booming in the small tavern, and the guy went sailing backwards. Then Frank grabbed the drunken man in front of him and started slamming punches into his face, his heart, and his stomach, finishing the job he'd started a few minutes ago.

Frank was starting to enjoy himself again, especially when the drunken guy was handed an empty whiskey bottle by one of his cohorts.

Having the bottle in his hand gave the guy all kinds of crazy self-confidence.

"You bastard, you're gonna be sorry now," he said, waving the bottle over his head the way an Injun would swing a tomahawk.

Frank just grinned. This bastard really was nuts.

The first thing Frank did was sail a right cross into the guy's face, breaking his nose. Blood gushed out like an oil strike. The second thing Frank did was grab the empty bottle from the drunk's hand. The third thing Frank did was lay that bottle against the man's cranium in a most unfriendly way. The fourth thing Frank did was grab his own revolver from the bar and aim it in the general vicinity of the thugs.

"Any one of you boys want some of this?"

They stood there smelling pretty bad and snarling with all the venom of stage villains, but not one of them was fool enough to tangle with Frank. He was getting a little crazy himself now, as the drunk crumpled at his feet demonstrated. Frank had pounded him a little harder than was necessary and maybe took a little too much pleasure in it. Frank was starting to enjoy hurting people, and they all knew it.

The bartender was back behind the bar now. "You shouldn't have ought to have hurt my brother so much," he said.

"Yeah, I guess I shouldn't ought to have. He seemed like such a nice, sweet fella." Frank backed out the door, gun ready, fury still dark in his gaze.

He was ready to finish his trip to Kelly Bay, where tomorrow he'd meet up with his brother David of the Royal Canadian Mounted Police. He didn't want anything else to hamper his trip. When he got outside, he scattered all the horses, then he mounted his own and rode fast into the chill, dark night.

chapter
five

TWELVE YEARS AGO, DAVID ADAMS, THEN JUST
a recruit in the Royal Canadian Mounted Police, became
good friends with another recruit, a young man from Hudson
Bay named Karl Swenson. As constables, the men shared
their first three assignments: the first raiding the fortress of
the province's largest whiskey bootlegger, the second locat-
ing the bones of men who had been lost in a snowstorm the
previous winter, and the third helping two medical men
stem the worst of a small cholera outbreak. By this time,
they were real Mounties, not just recruits.

After two years of this, including a six-month period
when they'd both been stationed at the same post, Swenson
decided he wanted to settle down, raise a family, and find
a job that paid real money. The seventy-five cents a day
offered by the Mounties just wasn't enough.

During this time, Adams had been seeing a young woman
named Anna Rolvig, but after a time it became obvious to
both that while they liked each other a great deal, they had
little in common, and the prospect for a lasting romance was
dim. After a few months, Swenson began seeing Anna. Not
only did they have their Swedish heritage in common, they
also both wanted the same things and wanted them soon: a
respectable middle-class life including children, and a job
that offered financial security.

21

So Swenson left the force. Adams didn't hear from him for nearly five years, and then one day a letter arrived saying that Swenson had become vice president of the bank in Kelly Bay. He had married Anna three years earlier, and she now carried their second child.

Swenson, as unreliable a correspondent as Adams himself, soon let his wife write the letters. She kept Adams informed of everything: the new baby, the death of the bank president, Karl's appointment to the position, and the building of their fine, new home.

The letters were occasional, but they were always warm and informative, and the invitation for David to come up to Kelly Bay and stay with the Swensons was quite genuine.

Then came the letter telling Adams of Karl's suicide and of the fiery way he chose to end his life. Adams read it all in disbelief. Why would a man do something like this? Particularly a man who'd always seemed as stable as Karl Swenson?

Anna wrote Adams a few more brooding letters following Karl's death, but then the correspondence ended. An investigation by local law enforcement was launched, but nothing was really turned up. The investigation was hampered by the worst series of blizzards in the past two decades, with most of the area virtually shut down for two months.

The next letter was from Adams to Anna. He said that on Wednesday, April 19, he was to meet his brother Frank at Kelly Bay's small Mountie post and would then stop in to visit Anna. As friends of the dead man, the brothers were determined to find out what had happened to him in the last months of his life.

"There wasn't any kind of warning?" David asked.
"He started acting kind of . . . funny, I guess."
"Anything you could put your finger on?"

"Well," Anna said, after the meal had been finished and the two girls dispatched upstairs to get ready for bed, "you know how Karl was. He kept to himself mostly, and he was usually brooding about something." She shook her head. "But it was hard to tell what was going on in his mind."

"His job was going well?"

"Pretty well—except for the robbery."

"Robbery?"

"The bank was held up not long before he died, but that could happen to anybody." She frowned. "They never did catch the thieves."

The robbery interested David, but he decided to go on with his other questions.

"And his health was good?" David said.

"As far as I knew."

His next question made him uncomfortable. "And your marriage?"

She dropped her gaze. That in itself said something. "It was fine."

But obviously she wasn't telling him everything. They sat for long moments in embarrassed silence.

He looked around the house, at the crackling yellow fire in the wide, brick fireplace, at the soft shadows the fire cast across the large, comfortable living room, at the somber portrait of Karl in his Sunday best, brooding in one shadowy corner. He looked to be a very different man from the enthusiastic but somewhat raw Mountie constable he'd been. Success had not only added fifteen pounds to the man, it had also given him a faint air of self-importance. A white fluffy cat sat on the couch, every once in a while raising her head to look at the portrait with a certain disdain.

"I wish it was easier for me to talk," Anna said.

"I shouldn't have asked the question. I'm sorry."

"But I want to know why he did it, David. I won't be able to rest until I do." She hesitated. "Something had changed with him."

"Do you know what exactly?"

She glanced anxiously over at the staircase, as if afraid the girls might be coming downstairs again. She leaned forward and spoke in little more than a whisper. "In the last year of his life, we were man and wife only once."

She dropped her eyes again. This was difficult for her.

"Do you have any idea why?"

"No, not really." She touched long, graceful fingers to her cheek. "I'm not young any longer. I had the sense that he'd tired of me."

"I just can't believe that, Anna. You're as pretty as ever." And she was.

She smiled. "Thank you. I know it's vain of me, but it's nice to hear a compliment. It's been so long." She looked at him with the sad, dignified beauty of her blue gaze, one of those women whose sexuality is only enhanced by her sturdy respectability.

Then the girls came down the stairs, two little angels in flannel nightgowns, the hems hitting the arches of their little pink feet. They ran over to their mother and clung to her the way they had this afternoon, eager for another glimpse of the stranger in the bright red coat with the golden buttons, but too shy to look at him without clutching their mother.

Anna had each of them give Uncle David a kiss, and then she excused herself and took the girls upstairs to be tucked in. While he waited, David went over to the fire, letting the front of him get very warm while his backside remained cool.

Men had a way of changing. The boy you grow up with will likely become a stranger to you by the time he reaches manhood. And there was no reason to think that Karl Swenson would have been any different. He'd come to Kelly Bay filled with the raw dreams common to poor young men in all the provinces—a wife, respectability, success—but in achieving them, he'd likely changed a great deal. Adams's eyes fixed on the portrait again. Yes, this was a different man from the young constable. There was a definite sense of a preening self-confidence here, even a hint of arrogance.

"He was a handsome man."

He hadn't heard her come down the stairs.

Now he turned to her, and before he quite knew what was happening, she was in his arms, clinging to him just the way her two daughters had clung to her, for understanding and protection and love. She began to sob, raw, choking sounds that made him feel helpless and vaguely afraid, and she did not let go of him for a very long time.

She looked up at him, then, her arms still around his waist, and said, "I just want to know why he did it, David. Please help me find out. Please."

And then she fell to sobbing again, and all Adams could do was dumbly hold her until she finished. Then he helped her over to the couch, where she lay down and went immediately to sleep. He found a blanket in the closet and covered her with it, then he let himself out.

chapter
six

AN HOUR AND A HALF AFTER MYRA LIVERMORE
left her office, she returned. By now, her house was reaching its peak for the night, the player piano pounding out
one tune after another, the girls looking good and clean
and eager, the customers at just the right stage of drink, the
stage where they could have fun without getting rowdy or
sick or melancholy. Myra didn't care much for men at all,
but she cared even less for drunken men.

When she opened the door, she saw the mortician, Richard
Harkin, tucked in a shadowy corner, eager but still looking
slightly ashamed of himself for wanting the things he wanted.
She closed the door behind her, her plump, damp hands
covering the doorknob as she leaned back and stared at
Richard.

"Everything's ready."

His head shot up. She saw the way his eyes gleamed.

That was the secret to a successful house—have that one
special thing that they can't get anywhere else. And then,
just stand back and watch how much they'll pay. It was
part funny and part disgusting, the way men were.

"You take a bath tonight, Richard?"

"Yes, ma'am."

"You telling me the truth, Richard?"

"Yes, ma'am."

"You got any weapons on you?"

"No, ma'am."

"Not even a knife?"

"No, ma'am. Not even a knife."

"You been drinking tonight?"

"You said not to, ma'am, so I didn't."

"You remember them rules I told you, Richard?"

"Yes, ma'am?"

"Can you repeat them?"

"Yes, ma'am. Rule number one is that there ain't to be no violence of any kind. Rule number two is that I'm to leave peaceful-like the minute you knock on the door."

He seemed to hesitate, so she said, "And rule number three?"

"That there ain't to be no light on. Not under any circumstances."

"That's right."

"Ma'am?"

"What?"

"How come that is, about the light and all?"

"You want to go up there?"

"Oh, yes; yes, ma'am, indeed I do."

"Then you abide by my rules and keep your goddamn questions to yourself."

"Yes, ma'am."

"Now you follow me."

"Yes, ma'am."

He picked up his black derby, playing with it nervously in his long, bony fingers, and followed her out of the room.

Nobody paid them any attention as they ascended the stairs. Everybody was too busy.

She took him to the second floor, then the third, then all the way down the hallway to where the attic door was. By

now, he was trembling and drool glistened in the corner
of his mouth. His dark eyes still shone with shame. No
doubt about it, Myra Livermore thought. Men sure were
disgusting animals.

She took out the key, held it up to his eyes. She saw
the way his body tensed, then trembled again. She loved
to tease him.

She took the key and bent over and inserted it into the
lock. From the floor below them came a shriek of laughter.

He jerked, as if somebody had discharged a firearm.

"You ready?" she said.

"Yes, ma'am."

"You remember them rules?"

"Yes, ma'am."

She nodded her head, turned the key, then stood back as
the door eased open on its own.

Ahead of him was a pitch black cave. You couldn't even
see the stairs from here.

"If you're gonna go, get goin' now," Myra said, shooing
him into the dark doorway the way she'd shoo an animal.

"Yes'm," he said, scurrying across the space between
them.

He went inside, put out a lone tentative foot in search of
a step, and then seemed to stumble forward for a moment.
Then he found the step, turned around to look at Myra and
gave her a sorrowful grin.

She didn't return the smile at all. Instead, she pushed the
door shut, locked it quickly, then walked away.

On the way down the stairs, she checked the railroad
watch she kept in the folds of her dress. When you bought
the attic, you never bought more than twenty minutes. She
always made sure of that.

She went to her office and had some brandy, then wondered which of the girls she'd sleep with later tonight.

chapter
seven

MYRA HAD A CERTAIN WAY OF PICKING HER OWN girl for the evening.

She'd go upstairs to where they were all scurrying around getting ready for the customers, and she'd make it real obvious that she had a small diamond or jewel in her hand. The girls would see the gift she planned to give to her paramour tonight, and they'd then start snuggling up to Myra in a way that was almost sickening. They'd flatter her, and they'd touch her dyed hair, or they'd stroke the organdy of her dress—all just so they could catch her eye.

This amused Myra greatly. She believed that all people could be bought if you just offered them something they really wanted; the ways the girls acted when they saw her little gifts was proof of this.

Myra stood in the doorway of one of the rooms now, watching three half-naked girls hurry with the last of their rouge. There was one little farmgirl from Peoria, Illinois, whom Myra had yet to sample, so she kept her eye closely on her.

The girl, Ida, smiled in the mirror at Myra as the older woman held up the diamond between her thumb and forefinger and displayed it for a moment. Myra returned the smile.

The other two girls frowned. They realized that Myra had made her choice for the evening. They helped each other with their dresses and quickly scurried from the room, leaving Myra and the farmgirl.

Myra lit a cheroot, spat the end of it into a nearby wastebasket, and then walked over to where Ida was just now pulling up her corset, her full breasts looking even more sumptuous as they were pushed together.

"You look real nice tonight, Ida," Myra said, her eyes fixed on Ida's breasts.

"Thank you, Miss Myra." She started shaping her dark hair with the help of a comb and brush.

"You like to drink bourbon?"

Ida looked as if Myra had just asked her a trick question. Her blue eyes got real cagey, and she said, "I'm always careful to water the drinks, Miss Myra. The way you say to. I never get drunk."

"How about afterward, when the girls are sitting around? Do you get drunk then?"

"Oh, once in awhile, I guess."

Myra took a step closer, slid her hand over the gentle slope of Ida's hip.

"Would you ever consider getting drunk with me?"

Ida smiled at Myra in the mirror. "I suppose I could be talked into it."

Myra raised the diamond for the girl to see. "Would this help make up your mind?"

The girl laughed harshly. "Miss Myra, you sure know how to talk sweet to a girl."

"You've got a nice body."

"Thank you, Miss Myra."

"Nice long legs." Myra licked her lips. "And nice young breasts."

But the girl wasn't paying any attention. She just kept staring at the diamond in Myra's fingers.

The girl turned around abruptly then, and said, "Would you hand me my dress over there, Miss Myra?"

"I'd be happy to."

Ida's dress was draped over a chair. Myra picked up the taffeta gown and brought it over to Ida. Ida slipped it over her head and snugged it down over her body. No doubt about it, this farm girl was one of the best-looking whores Myra had ever had in her house.

"Any special kind of bourbon you like?" Myra said.

"What kind do you have?"

" 'Bout any kind you want, darlin'."

"My daddy was always partial to sourmash."

"Nobody can say a bad word about sourmash in my presence."

"That sounds good, then, Miss Myra."

Ida surprised her by sliding her arm around Myra's thickening waist.

"Miss Myra?" the girl asked seductively.

"Yes?"

"Can I see it one more time before I go downstairs tonight?"

"See what?" Myra loved to tease.

"You know."

"The diamond, you mean?"

"Yes, Miss Myra, the diamond."

And when Myra held it up, she felt the girl begin to go weak, almost collapse against her.

The close proximity to this tender young flesh stirred Myra.

"It's so beautiful, Miss Myra."

"You're beautiful, too, you know that?" Myra said.

She kissed the girl on the lips and then pushed her gently away. "You get downstairs and make some money for Miss Myra, all right?"

"I'll make you a lot of money tonight, Miss Myra. I promise."

And with that, Ida hurried out of the room and down the stairs.

Myra smiled to herself. She almost felt sorry for these young girls. They were so goddamn dumb it was pathetic; they didn't even know the difference between real diamonds and cheap imitations. Tonight, Ida was going to give herself to Myra for nothing more than a dime-store paste imitation. How much dumber could you get?

chapter
eight

I Escaped From the Grave
Crooked Clergymen
How a Coterie of Villains Amuse Themselves in Prison

"GOOD TO SEE YOU'RE STILL READING GREAT literature," David Adams said the next morning as he walked into the small log cabin at the Mountie outpost.

His brother Frank—thickset where David was slim, dark haired where David was blond, given to gunplay where David was given to talk—looked up and smiled.

"You can keep Shakespeare," he said. He tapped the magazine he was reading. "I'll take *The Police Gazette* any day."

The outpost here consisted of two log cabins and three Mounties. David was bedding down in the barracks during his stay in Kelly Bay. He'd arranged for Frank to bunk here, too.

David had just been down to the creek for an early morning swim. The chilly water had managed to provide a cleansing bath, too.

"You ready for some breakfast?" David said.

"It's not Mountie food, is it? Canned stew and dry powder biscuits?"

"I wouldn't think that a man who read *The Police Gazette*

33

would be fussy about his food," David said. "Anyway, the old man *liked* Mountie food, you'll remember."

Invoking their father left both men silent for a moment. Their old man had been one of the Mounties' first officers. He'd been stabbed to death in his sleep by a whiskey runner. His sons had tracked the man down and killed him. David had carried on the tradition by donning a red coat, but Frank had elected to be a U.S. Marshal working in Montana and along the border. Because David also worked along the border, the two brothers saw each other frequently, as now.

David said, "I'm told there's a good restaurant in the business district. It's not exactly close, but it's a nice spring morning, and a walk'll do you good."

He patted playfully at the extra weight his older brother had put on in the belly. Frank had a fondness for drinking beer and playing poker, neither of which kept one in shape.

Frank waggled his copy of *The Police Gazette.* "All right if I bring this along? There's a really interesting story about a man who ate an alligator."

David didn't catch the joke at first, but then he suddenly burst out laughing and slapped his brother on the back. "I'm just glad to know you don't take that rag seriously."

"Just like a little fun, brother. Just like a little fun."

They set off walking into Kelly Bay as Frank told his brother about the brawl he'd had at a tavern last night. "I thought you told me these Canadians were peaceful folks." He laughed. He enjoyed baiting Frank about the so-called peaceful Canadians.

The idea had come to Robinson in the middle of the night. He'd awakened, the smells of Myra Livermore's whorehouse raw in the darkness—whiskey, cigar smoke, perfume—and thought: Of course, that's where the money is. Under the bridge where he always went fishing.

He wanted to bolt from bed right then—he slept on a cot in the basement, his mulatto blood precluding him from sleeping on the same floor as white people, even if those people happened to be prostitutes—but he knew better. If he got up on his feet to sneak out the door, Myra would hear him.

Sometimes, he thought that old bitch was positively supernatural in her ability to hear him come and go. No matter what time he came in at night, she said, "Where'd you go cattin' around last night?"

And no matter how silently he crept out to visit the colored camp down near the bay, she heard that, too, and she'd smile her harsh knowing smile in the morning and say, "You were out samplin' some of that dark poontang last night, weren't you, Robinson?" Then she'd grin all the more and say, "You know, Robinson, for a one-eyed half-nigger of fifty-three, you sure get your share of pussy."

To which he always wanted to reply, "Then that's something we have in common, Myra, cause you sure get your share of pussy, too."

Now he walked out the front door, and he was whistling because it was eight in the morning on a sunny day, and he was just setting off for town as he always set off for town, and there was no reason at all for Myra Livermore to get suspicious. Against the side of the house leaned a new bicycle. He'd saved four paychecks to buy it. Myra didn't pay for shit, but it was more than he used to make as a field hand back in Georgia before the war.

He took his bike and set off.

The closer he got to Kelly Bay, the more people he saw, meaning more white people. How they smiled every time they saw Robinson on his bicycle. He wasn't a bad-looking man—tall, with a coffee-colored face that some might regard as handsome, wearing a black eyepatch over the eye socket a vigilante mob had cleaned out with a knife. He always wore clean clothes, always bathed. He was at least as well-spoken as half the people who lived in the Bay, and for the most part, folks here treated him with a kind of abrupt courtesy, as if they didn't want to be rude, but then they didn't want to stand too close to a mulatto either, on the off-chance that they might catch something.

All this, Robinson was used to. It was the standard way white people treated black people. It was when he boarded his bicycle that he had got his feelings hurt. Because whenever a white person of any age—kids were just as bad as their parents—saw him aboard his bike, they smirked. And it was a mendacious, superior smirk, one that crushed Robinson every time he saw it, a smirk that said, Now what's a nigger doing on a bicycle? As if he were some kind of circus monkey.

So this morning, he put his head down.

He watched the rough dirt road carefully so he wouldn't spill his bike. But he didn't look at the faces. Oh, he was aware of people passing him—he saw shiny shoes and the hems of skirts and walking canes tamping the ground—but he kept his vision low so he wouldn't have to see the smirks. And he whistled to himself so he wouldn't have to hear the giggles and the titters and the laughter.

He just kept saying to himself, I'm going to find that money, and I'm going to get out of this place, and I'm going to go someplace with my money where I won't be a nigger any more. Yes, sir, I'm going to find that place and live the rest of my life out there.

Breakfast was two things: heaping plates full of sliced potatoes, easy-over eggs, thick slices of bacon, steaming cups of coffee; and David's story of their old friend Karl Swenson.

They sat in a small, smoky restaurant packed with grizzled men who spoke mostly French. These were the traders and trappers who worked the wilderness that lay between settlements and towns. Many of them had carried their rifles inside, unwilling to go unarmed even in a restaurant. They had little more than contempt for the Mounties; Mounties had too often broken up their profitable relationships supplying whiskey and guns to bands of renegade Indians. To them, a good Mountie was a dead Mountie, being lowered six feet into God's own earth while a Canadian flag flapped overhead.

But after a time, they lost interest in the Mountie and went back to their meals.

Frank said, "So his wife said he changed?"

David nodded. "And that's what we need to find out— what happened to him in the last months of his life."

"Maybe he took the bank robbery personally."

"I thought of that, too," David said. "A proud man like Karl—and apparently he got a lot prouder when he became bank president—might see the robbery as some kind of reflection on himself."

Frank said, "Then there's always the possibility of another woman."

"Not Karl."

Frank shrugged. "It happens. Especially to men who suddenly get successful, the way Karl did. They start to feel powerful, and they want to impress somebody with their power. Their wives know too much about them to be impressed, and so they start looking elsewhere."

David thought of the man's portrait in the front room. The arrogance he'd seen in the eyes and mouth, the arrogance put there since Karl Swenson had moved to Kelly Bay and become an important man.

"I guess you're right." He sipped coffee. "Anyway, I thought that with two of us asking questions, we could probably get some kind of bead on what happened."

Frank shook his head and grimaced. "He sure as hell must have started hating himself, setting himself on fire the way he did."

"That's what I keep thinking," David said. "What the hell could have caused him to do it?"

The men finished their meals, left money on the table, and left the restaurant.

chapter
nine

ORIGINALLY, KELLY BAY WAS TWO SMALL COM-
munities: one on the west end, one on the east. There were
the usual differences found on the frontier—the east end
tended to be Presbyterian, the west end to be Lutheran—
and there were also curious discrepancies in soil content.
The soil of the east end of the bay seemed to be better
for crops, while the soil on the west seemed better for
grazing. While there was no ready scientific explanation
for this—hell, the two ends of the Bay were at most a
half-mile apart—locals insisted that this was so and acted
accordingly.

Then came a Mountie named McPhearson, a wry strapping
man who was quite the bare-knuckle fighter after two or
three samples of homebrew, and one day McPhearson told
them how crazy they were, living in a partitioned fashion
this way.

McPhearson convinced nobody at first. Only gradually,
after visiting Kelly Bay again and again on his swing west,
did he finally get representatives from both sides of the
town to sit down and discuss things in a civilized manner.

Eight years and many bare-knuckle exhibitions after he
began preaching the gospel according to McPhearson, the
Mountie finally persuaded the two sides to come together
and build a bridge connecting the east and west. Not just a
simple little connecting bridge, either, but one wide enough

for two stagecoaches to cross simultaneously and sturdy enough to hold up for a good half a century, a wooden truss bridge with iron tie rods and wrought-iron construction. And so the bridge was built, and not surprisingly, it was known as McPhearson's Bridge, though the Mountie in question had many years ago gone to that big barracks in the sky.

Robinson used to bring his bike up to the bridge and ride across it. He liked the way the planks rumbled beneath his wheels, and he liked the clean, cool wind that came off the water, and he liked the sense of motion he had when he looked down at the rushing water.

On so fine a day as this one, at least a dozen fishermen were hard at work, lines already extended deep into the sparkling blue waters of the bay. There were boys with freckles and cowlicks and respectable merchants with clean celluloid collars and rough but friendly workingmen, and all there had one thing in common: they were all playing hooky. Each should have been in school or behind a cash register or wielding a hammer—but who could study or work on the first good fishing day of the year?

Robinson sat on top of the hill watching them, his right leg slung casually over the bar on his bike. Hell, there was no need to be nervous. They wouldn't know what he was up to. They'd just think that he was one more strange nigger doing some strange nigger things.

He got back on his bike, and coasted down the hill to McPhearson Bridge.

He leaned his bicycle against the bridge railing and scrambled down the rocky incline to the shore. He could hear the white folks talking about him, some with curiosity, some with amusement, some with that quick sharp anger that always amazed him with its heat. He kept scrambling till he reached the water.

Every spring, dead fish from downstream washed up here. The smell was pretty bad today. He turned around and started walking back toward the bridge, waving to the white folks who watched him. Most waved lazily back. He just wanted to assure them that he was just as dumb and shiftless as they all thought. He decided to give them the whole show, the big *shucks* grin and the big *shucks* wave, both of which said that he was content to be just what he was, and that they certainly had nothing to fear from him.

Once he got under the bridge where nobody could see him, he put his middle finger up in the air and whispered a few words to himself that his mama would never have approved of. Then he set to work.

He put great stock in his dream because he put great stock in premonitions. When he was fourteen years old, he'd gotten a nice plump mulatto girl pregnant. Her people were very angry, and one of her brothers cut Robinson's back up pretty good with a knife. But Robinson had told them not to fear, that the child would be born dead. He'd had a dream, Robinson had, even back then, and he had faith in his dream.

The baby was born six months early—dead, as Robinson had predicted.

Robinson had recently had another dream, and he planned to collect on it.

He searched for half an hour under the bridge before he found what he was looking for. Just where the land and the bottom of the bridge joined, there was a heavy piece of scrap iron that looked as if it had been left behind by the engineers. It took Robinson ten minutes to push it a foot and a half.

The ground was damp where the scrap iron had been, and two wet, pink nightcrawlers wriggled out of their holes beneath.

There was nothing to be suspicious of unless you had come here suspicious. Robinson got down on his hands and knees and searched every inch of the ground under this side of the bridge. He found nothing. Only the piece of scrap iron could possibly conceal something. Only the dirt beneath the iron was worth his suspicion.

He set to work again. He hadn't dared bring a shovel. That certainly would have caused the white folks to wonder what he was doing.

He took a careful look around, decided that he was alone, and set to work. He used his hands, and even though the nails started bleeding, he kept right on using his hands. One thing being a slave had taught him was toleration for pain. His toleration soon enough paid off.

He had dug maybe three feet down before he felt it, but once his fingers touched it, he knew for certain he'd found what he was looking for. And then he did a most peculiar thing, Robinson did. He covered the hole back up, then he pushed the scrap iron back over the hole, and he just sat there laughing.

He knew they could hear him upside but he didn't care. They'd just say, "There goes that dumb nigger again laughin' his fool head off." And then they'd just forget all about him.

He sat there for a long time, Robinson did, thinking about all the ways he was going to spend the money. Then he thought about the attic, and his laughter stopped abruptly.

He didn't like to think about the attic because it always depressed him. Sometimes he'd lay there at night and imagine he could hear the sounds coming from the attic, and they'd sicken him. Sometimes he'd want to get his Henry rifle and go up there and just start shooting. Sometimes he'd—

Now, he just shook his head, sat back, and tried to think again of all the things the money could buy him. Freedom, real freedom, for the first time in his life. Women and good food and smart hotels and—

But no matter how hard he tried, Robinson couldn't quit thinking about the attic.

He would definitely have to deal with the attic before he took the money and fled town. He was going to have to do it.

Five minutes later, Robinson was on his bicycle again and heading toward town.

chapter
ten

AS HE MOVED AROUND TOWN ASKING QUES-
tions, Frank Adams noticed how well laid out the telegraph
wires were.

As in the frontier west, the telegraph had brought civiliza-
tion to frontier Canada, though not everybody was pleased
with the appearances of hundreds of telegraph poles and
the buzzing wires strung between them. A few decades
ago, there had been a kind of vigilante team that had gone
through the backwoods, chopping down poles in the dead
of night. They considered this means of "communicating
by lightning" a form of deviltry and wanted nothing to do
with it.

Still others saw it as a hoax. There was the case of a man
who received a telegraph note from his best friend—but the
man refused to believe the friend had written it because the
note was not in the friend's handwriting.

In America, some people refused to believe the results of
the 1848 presidential election because they first heard the
results over the telegraph wire and figured it was a trick by
the Whigs to promote their candidate, Zachary Taylor.

But even when the people were enthusiastic about the
telegraph, problems remained. Wires continually broke,
operators were often inexperienced and thus incompetent,
and the equipment was poor until much later in the century.

Eventually, though, the telegraph operator became one of the most envied people in town. He knew many of the towns-people's secrets and so became a god-like figure to some.

Frank had long ago learned that if you wanted to find something out about a particular town, the best man to talk to was the telegraph operator.

"So you knew Karl Swenson?" Frank asked.

"Yep."

"You saw him often?"

"Yep."

"You talk to him much?"

"Yep."

"He ever discuss his private life?"

"Yep."

"You have any idea why he would have killed himself like that?"

"Yep."

"You think you could tell me why he did it?"

"Hmm. Don't rightly know, I guess."

The telegraph office was located on a corner of the main street's busiest intersection. The interior was very pleasant, with mahogany appointments, a service desk that ran from wall to wall with a section that folded back to let the opera-tor in and out, and what appeared to be the very latest model in telegraph equipment.

The operator was in his fifties, chunky, with a striking mane of grandfatherly white hair and a chaw of tobacco in his cheek that rivaled the size of a baseball. After saying "Yep," he frequently spat into a spitoon kept discreetly out of sight and not, one assumed, meant to be shared with mere customers.

Now, he looked carefully at Frank and said, "You say you're a marshal?"

Frank decided to talk the way the operator did. "Yep."

"And you say you're up here meeting your brother?"

"Yep."

"And you say he's a Mountie?"

"Yep."

"And you say he was a Mountie back when Karl Swenson was?"

"Yep."

"I'll be damned." The operator shook his head. "Always figured Karl was just makin' that up."

"Making what up?"

"About being a Mountie and all."

"Did Karl usually make things up?"

"No. But he was kind of boastful, if you know what I mean. Liked to impress people."

"What did he like to boast about?"

"Hell, everything. Liked to show off his new duds and liked to show off his new surrey and liked to let you know about his women."

"What women?"

"Well, if you knew much about Karl, then you knew he had an eye for the ladies."

"Oh?"

"And the ladies had an eye for him."

"Any ladies in particular?"

"Woman named Liz Conway."

"They were friendly?"

The operator winked at him. "Very friendly."

"How do you know that?"

"Karl came in one night late, wanted to send a telegram. He had a snootful, too, let me tell you."

"And he mentioned Liz Conway?"

"Didn't need to mention her. I saw her out in the surrey. His surrey."

"I see."

"She's a beauty."

"Liz is?"

"Yep. And she's a widow. You know how they are."

"No. How are they?"

"Man hungry."

"Guess maybe I'll have to find myself a widow woman."

"Hell, if I was your age, Marshal Adams, they'd be the first women I'd look up. Wear a fellow out."

"Is that right?"

"Aw, hell, yes. Everybody knows that."

"Where would I find this widow Conway?"

The operator gave him directions. "You goin' out there?"

"Sounds like it."

The operator winked at him. "You won't be sorry."

"You sure?"

"Sure I'm sure." He jabbed himself in the chest with a thumb. "One thing I know about it's widow women. Why, when I was your age, son, I specialized in 'em."

Frank laughed. "I guess maybe you did at that."

He tugged his hat down and turned to the door. Then he looked back at the operator. "Any other women Karl was running around with in particular?"

In particular, I'd say it was just the Conway woman."

"Well, thanks. I appreciate it."

The operator grinned and spat tobacco, then swung his eyes back to Frank. "You better get yourself a good night's sleep, Marshal. With Liz, you're gonna need it, believe me."

Frank laughed. "Well, thanks for the advice, old-timer."

He went out to the street again.

chapter
eleven

DAVID FELT AS IF HE HAD JUST STEPPED INSIDE a church. The interior was so hushed, the people so proper, he half-expected to see a minister come out and greet him.

The bank was two large rooms. Along the left wall were three teller cages; along the right wall were three desks. In the back, in the second room, two large, glass-enclosed offices had been partitioned off. In one of them, fitted into the rear wall, was the steel door to the vault. The paneling throughout was expensive mahogany, and the carpeting was deep, plush, and wine-colored.

David noted that there was a pecking order here. All the employees wore celluloid collars and high-button cassimere suits. They also wore wireless glasses and some kind of glossy preparation on their center-parted hair. Their smiles were quick but cold.

One such man, noting David's uniform, came out to greet the Mountie. He had a fussy little mustache and a somewhat arch manner. "May I help you?"

"I'd like to see the bank president."

"You have an appointment?"

"I'm afraid not."

"He's very busy today." The man leaned in and half-whispered, "Mrs. Muldoon."

"Mrs. Muldoon?"

"Our largest depositer."

"I see." David was polite enough not to ask if Mrs. Muldoon was the largest depositer in the sense that she had the most money here, or the largest in the sense that she was the fattest. Perhaps she could lay claim to both. "I'd only need a few minutes."

The man looked anxiously at the door, then raised nervous brown eyes to the Ingram clock tocking away high up on the wall. "Well, she isn't due for another fifteen minutes. I suppose that—"

Just then a man who looked very much like all the other employees only more so—his collar a little whiter, his suit a little more expensive, his hair a little slicker—peeked out from the biggest office in the rear and said, "Mayhew?"

The man next to David said, "Yes sir, coming." Then to David, "Excuse me. That's Mr. Rafferty, the president."

As Mayhew walked to the back of the bank, he passed two young women to whom he half-bowed. He looked like a young boy imitating something he'd seen an adult do, his bow awkward and clearly embarrassing to the young women. Mayhew apparently suffered under the illusion that he was a ladies' man.

He was gone a minute and a half. David timed him on the big Ingram.

When he came back, he leaned even closer to David, smelling sweetly of after-shave, and said in a whisper, "He says you're making people nervous. He says you're to come into his office."

David wanted to point out that Mounties didn't ordinarily take orders from bank people, not even exalted bank presidents themselves, that there was in fact a carefully conceived Mountie hierarchy from whom he took orders—but why upset Mayhew?

• • •

"I'm afraid your coat disturbs people."

"Oh."

"They see a red coat, and they think Mountie. And when they think Mountie, they think trouble."

"I see."

"And when they think trouble, they get nervous. They start thinking about their money in the vault, and is it really safe and all, and then they start asking me a lot of foolish questions that I can't answer, such as, Will the bank ever be robbed again?, and Is Canadian currency going to collapse the way currency does in South American countries?, and, If there isn't any trouble, why is a Mountie with his red coat standing in our bank? You see what I'm talking about?"

"I think so."

His speech delivered, Mr. James T. Rafferty (that was how the fancy script letters on his door identified him, anyway) lunged across his wide desk and shook David's hand. He had a quick sharp grip, like the bite of a garter snake.

He sat back, steepled his fingers, and said, "So tell me, what *is* a Mountie doing in our bank?"

"I want to ask you some questions about Karl Swenson."

"Oh." His voice lost its fervor and so did his eager brown eyes. Obviously, Karl Swenson was a topic second only to cholera in popularity. "The bank robbery."

"The robbery and some personal questions, too."

Rafferty sat back and hooked his thumbs into the flap pockets on his vest. "We're trying to put that particular era behind us."

"I'm sure you are."

"Karl was a nice man but he was—" Rafferty shrugged and dropped his eyes.

"He was what?"

Rafferty looked up again. "I'm going to say something that will probably come off as very snobbish to you." He cleared his throat, the way he probably did when speaking to his luncheon club, and said, "I don't think you should take a man from the lower orders and make him president of a bank."

"The lower orders?"

"Do you know what his father did?"

"His father was a farmer."

"Exactly my point. Karl hadn't been properly groomed or prepared for this job." A look of displeasure settled on Rafferty's angular face now; he was remembering something he'd rather forget. "When I was passed over for the presidency in favor of Karl, I—"

He stopped, seeing that he'd been too obvious in making his point.

"I didn't hold it against Karl, of course," he went on, his hollow cheeks dappled with red, "but I must say I was concerned for the bank when I learned that . . ." He paused, steepled his fingers again, and tried to look as if he just hated to say what he was about to say. "Karl, I'm afraid, was not a very good family man."

"No?"

"No. For one thing, he and a young woman who worked here became . . . familiar. So familiar, that the Board of Directors had to let her go."

"I see."

"And that wasn't all." He shook his head. He looked like a hanging judge now, the pure pleasure of mendacity obvious in his eyes and on his petulant lips. "When he knew that the Board of Directors were on to him—and eventually they caught on to everything, including Liz Conway—he started sneaking around at night. So nobody would find out. Or so he thought. He even started going to Myra Livermore's."

"What's that?"

"Just about the most vile house of sin in the entire territory. My wife blushes if we even so much as pass by the place."

"Heavens," David said, but the banker didn't seem to catch his sarcasm. "I suppose you have proof of this?"

"Oh, yes. Irrefutable proof. One of Myra's whores came into the bank three days before he killed himself."

"How do you know she was here to see him?"

He leaned forward. Now there was glee in his eyes. This was the part he genuinely relished. This was the part that got his juices flowing. "She walked right into his office, right in the middle of a meeting he was having with one of our directors, and slapped him very hard across the mouth. She shouted, 'You did it again last night, and you promised you wouldn't.'"

"Then what happened?"

"She stormed out. I've never seen this place in such a tizzy. All the respectable women turned their heads, of course. They didn't even want to look at the hussy."

"What did Swenson do?"

"What could he do? He closed the door and began appealing to Mr. Totten—the bank director I mentioned, and one of the elders of my church. I could see him through the glass, Swenson I mean. Pleading with Mr. Totten, pleading with him. The entire display was disgusting, let me tell you."

"What did Totten do?"

"He called a director's meeting for that very night."

"And the meeting came off?"

"Yes. That very night." He leaned back. He seemed sated now. David found it easy to imagine this prissy bastard in his churchly attire, affixing scarlet A's on the heads of women he considered sinful, and smiting men with his whining New Testament voice. "They were going to let him go."

"They took a vote?"

"Yes. Six to three."

"You said they were going to. Does that mean that they didn't actually fire him that night?"

"One of the directors, a very emotionally unstable man if you ask me, requested that everybody be given a week to cool off. He talked about all the wondrous things Swenson had done."

"Had he done some wondrous things?"

"Well, I suppose I have to give him the fact that during his tenure our assets increased ten times."

"Ten times? That's incredible, I'd say."

"Well, I suppose it's not bad," Rafferty said.

"Somebody told Karl of their decision, I suppose?"

Rafferty smiled. "I took the responsibility for that."

"How kind of you."

Rafferty's eyes narrowed. This time he'd definitely picked up on the sarcasm. "I was only doing my job."

"The woman from Myra's who came in here."

"What about her?"

"She said, 'You did it again last night and you promised you wouldn't.' Do you have any idea what she was talking about?"

"No, and I don't care to contemplate it."

"Do you happen to know her name?"

"Whose name?"

"The woman from Myra's."

"Of course not. How would somebody like me know her name?"

"I guess you've got a point there."

"I've never been to such a place in my life."

David smiled and stood up. He put his hand out. Rafferty again inflicted his sharp dog-bite of a grasp on David's.

"I'm just kind of curious . . ." David continued.

"About what?"

"You said that during Karl's tenure the assets went up ten times."

"Right."

"How much have they gone up during your first six months?"

"They told you, didn't they?"

"Told me?"

Rafferty nodded. "That the assets have gone down the last three months."

"No, nobody told me that."

"Well, it's just a temporary thing, I'm sure. I'm positive, in fact."

"I'm sure that's all it is," David said, unable to stop himself from smiling. "Temporary."

chapter
twelve

HER NAME WAS ROSARITA. SHE WAS SIXTY-SEVEN years old. She had been born in Mexico long, long ago when the Spaniards still controlled large parts of it. She had no precise idea of how she'd gotten to Canada, or even when. Rosarita had a curse, a whiskey curse, and if you kept her in whiskey, she did not ask questions.

Anyway, Rosarita had somewhere, somehow met Myra Livermore and become her cleaning woman. She didn't blanch at cleaning up blood on those nights when a girl had gotten cut, she didn't blanch at vomit on those nights when the customers drank more than their ample bellies would allow, and she didn't blanch at abuse. Everybody abused Rosarita. Myra cursed her, the girls laughed at her, the customers made fun of her. But she didn't care, not as long as she had enough whiskey to stay just so— just exactly right on the money, drunk but not too drunk. When she was at that point, she didn't give a damn about anything. She just did her work, scrubbing and dusting and waxing and polishing, and if called upon by Myra, she'd even go upstairs to a girl's room and part her legs and show her how to give herself a good customer-pleasing douche. Men, at least men who spent a lot of money, liked their women clean.

Only one thing about Myra's nice cozy set-up bothered

Rosarita, and that was the attic.

Rosarita always waited till Myra and the girls had gone out for the day before going up to the third floor and pressing her ear to the attic door. Like many whores, Myra's girls liked to go into town and flounce around, scandalizing the good Bible-toting ladies of the Bay, and driving wild those otherwise pure-hearted men married to the ladies. It was always fun to see a minister, a godly man after all, lick his lips when a painted whore passed by.

Now, Rosarita, standing just out of the dusty sunlight slanting through the northern window, leaned forward and pressed her ear to the attic door. She knew what was going on here. And even Rosarita, who had not made a confession to a *padre* in more than forty years, who had not taken the body and blood of Christ for at least as long, even Rosarita disapproved of what Myra was doing.

Anyway, couldn't Myra get arrested for doing such things? Even a lawman who'd been bought and paid for was likely to have an objection to this kind of going on.

Rosarita listened.

At this time of day, the house empty, about all you heard was the creak and crack of the house itself or one of the sweet little kitties who always seemed to be underfoot. Robinson was around sometimes, but he never bothered her. In fact, Robinson seemed to be afraid of her in some peculiar way. Some people were.

And then she heard it, what she'd heard the other times in the attic, the song. The name of it was "Dreaming Girl," and though Rosarita couldn't remember where or when she'd heard it the first time she certainly recalled the melody. It was so pretty and so sad at the same time that you just couldn't forget it, and somehow, though she could never explain it to anybody, the song seemed to be about Rosarita herself.

> *Dreaming girl*
> *Lost in the night*
> *Dreaming girl*
> *Praying for morn,*
> *Praying for light.*

The way the girl in the attic sang it made Rosarita cry, just the way it had the last time. She wondered so many things, Rosarita did: who the girl was, and how old she was, and where Myra had gotten her from, and what Myra planned to do with her.

The slap came from nowhere.

One moment, Rosarita had been standing at the attic door, listening, and then the next moment a pink fleshy hand of unbelievable speed and strength came chopping down through the air and struck Rosarita so hard that she was turned around and slammed against the wall.

Myra stood there, out of breath, florid with rage, spewing silver spittle all over Rosarita's face.

"You god damn wetback wino! You ever go near that door again, and I'll throw you out on your ass! Do you understand me?"

But at the moment, Rosarita couldn't understand anything. She sank to the floor and began sobbing. The slap had hurt so much and had been so disorienting. All she could think of was the song, "Dreaming Girl," and how it was about her and what had happened to her beauty and what had happened to her life. Then she thought of the girl in the attic, the girl who sang the sad song, and then without quite knowing why, she started crying all the harder.

Myra, ever the delicate flower, kicked Rosarita hard in the ribs and said, "You cheap Mexican cunt! Now you get up and get back to work, you hear me?"

Rosarita got up and got back to work.

chapter
thirteen

LIZ CONWAY WAS GOOD AT READING SIGNS AND portents. Her father had been a scout and so had taught her a variety of useful pieces of information.

She was standing at the sink when she heard the first faint sounds of an approaching horse. Given everything that had happened last night—she still had bruises on her arms and neck to prove how badly she'd been roughed up—she grabbed her carbine from the corner and ran out the door.

Frank Adams wasn't sure why, but he sensed that somebody was watching his approach to Liz Conway's cabin. He looked off the narrow trail to see if there was a safer way to reach Conway's. He halted his horse momentarily, then decided to ride up a steep but smooth hill lying a few hundred yards to the east. This way, he'd come up to the cabin at an angle nobody would expect.

As she crouched behind a wide, ragged granite boulder, her carbine held steady and ready, Liz thought again of last night.

What had the man been looking for? Who had sent him? Would he be bold enough to show up again today, in broad daylight?

She gripped her carbine, eager to use it.

As Frank crested the hill, he gazed below at a tidy if poor cabin that sat in the center of long grasses waving in the wind. Somebody had been cooking something recently. The smell of good meat charring was clean and tempting on the soft warm air.

But as pretty as the cabin and the grass and the winding stream of water looked, Frank sensed something wrong. Although he couldn't see anybody, he knew that somebody had anticipated his arrival and was waiting for him. He started slowly, warily down the hill.

Liz saw him angling down the steep hill. He wasn't the man from last night—he was too neatly dressed for that— but he was clearly a dangerous man.

She waited, eager to open fire.

chapter
fourteen

FRANK ADAMS DISMOUNTED, GROUND-TIED THE
dun he'd been riding since leaving Montana two and a
half weeks ago, and turned toward the small log cabin
just as the rifle fire cracked from behind a huge boulder
to his left.

Instinctively, the lawman pitched himself to the ground
and started rolling. The sniper would have to be damned
good to pick off a man who was moving as fast as Frank.
Rolling toward the cabin gave Frank time enough to draw
his .44 and start returning the gunfire.

The cabin sat on the edge of a small blue lake. The
land smelled of jackpine and buffalo grass. Two black
and white dairy cows stood outside a small shed down
by the lake, and a cardinal perched on an oak branch
just above Frank's head. In the higher, drier places to
the east of the cabin, he could see and smell bearberry,
blueberry, and woodland strawberry. Closer to the water,
he saw patches of juniper and dwarf dogwood. This was
still virgin territory out here. He wished he had time to stop
and appeciate it.

The gunfire boomed on the pastoral air of the setting.
Frank wondered who the hell was firing at him, and why.

Two more rifle shots cracked through the sweet morning air, and Frank didn't have time to wonder about any-

thing. All he could do was a little more rolling, and a little more firing of his own.

Now, out of breath, cursing himself for liking pancakes and fried food too well, he lay on the grass, waiting for the sniper to make his next move.

The boulder was half hidden by the thick, low-hanging branches of a jackpine. The sniper was amply hidden behind the foliage. And so, apparently, was the sniper's horse.

Frank was startled when he saw a red mare and a rider laid flat against the saddle suddenly charging out from behind the boulder.

The horse broke into a fast gallop. It rode straight at Frank, the metal shoes of its hooves flashing in the sunlight.

Frank barely had time to roll away from the course of the charging animal before being kicked by the flashing hooves. Frank rolled, but this time he also jumped to his feet, firing three warning shots low, only inches above the flat back of the retreating sniper.

Then Frank, whose father had always ragged him for being impulsive, did what few other sane people would even consider—he started running hard behind the horse, trying to not only outrun the mare but to reach up and grab the sniper and hurl him to the ground. Fortunately for Frank, the upslope was steep, and the horse was considerably slowed by it. The big mare kicked up chunks of turf that Frank had to duck as he grew closer, closer to the animal.

The sniper turned around once and tried to squeeze off a quick shot, but he had no leverage. Frank got a quick shot off himself, and the bullet slammed the Winchester from the sniper's hand.

Then Frank made his boldest move, coming abreast of the mare and jumping up to grab the sniper by the arm.

He felt the sleeve of the man's shirt start to tear away, then he felt the man's whole body start to pitch off the side of the horse. Frank gave a final jerk. The sniper came hurtling off his mount and pitched straight down into the earth, sprawling in an almost comic way on the grassy ground.

Not until Frank came a few steps closer, his .44 leveled straight at the sniper's spine, did he notice the soft curves of the sniper's body, and the long, lustrous dark hair that had come tumbling out from beneath the sniper's low-brimmed black hat.

"You bastard!" the sniper cried, rolling over to face Frank.

She was a woman all right, as her pleasantly full striped shirt revealed immediately. She was also a darned pretty woman in a green-eyed, angry sort of way.

"You may not know it, lady, but you were shooting at a U.S. lawman."

"Well, if you're a U.S. lawman what the hell are you doing up here in Canada?"

Frank chose not to answer that question. He'd accumulated a number of bumps and bruises in the course of knocking her off her mount, and the pain from the injuries made him irritable.

"I'm told Karl Swenson used to come out here."

"So, what if he did?"

"That's what I want to talk to you about."

"Well, what if I don't *want* to talk about it?"

Frank couldn't hold his temper any more. "What the hell's your problem, lady? I came to your cabin to talk to you, and you snuck out the back way and started firing at me."

"You ever think maybe I'm scared?" She stood there and glared at him.

Then she calmed down and looked faintly embarrassed. "Aw, hell. I got the wrong guy." She got to her feet with amazing agility, brushed the dirt off her considerably rounded body, then pointed back downslope to the cabin. "C'mon, Mr. Marshal, I'll treat you to a good glass of dandelion wine."

She hadn't been exaggerating the quality of the wine. Frank supposed he really shouldn't, being at least informally on duty and all, but as he sat at a wobbly wooden table inside the one-room log cabin, he was more caught up in the soft spring breeze through the open door—and the soft, sweet eyes of the woman—than he wanted to be.

She raised her glass and smiled. "I guess given what we've just been through, we need a little wine."

"You won't catch me arguin' about that."

He watched her drink, her long, graceful neck stretching slightly as she raised her face to meet the glass, and then when she finished, he raised his glass and she watched him drink.

"You curious about why I shot at you?"

He didn't quit drinking. One blue eye peeked around the edge of his glass. He nodded slightly.

"Because last night, somebody broke in here while I was asleep and darn near killed me. He really roughed me up."

Frank finished his wine. He was going to resist the temptation to ask for more. He was an honorable lawman—he always had the example of his father to follow, in case he tried to forget about being an honorable lawman—and so he said, "Any idea what he was looking for?"

"No. But it had something to do with a man I knew."

"Karl Swenson?"

"Right."

Frank watched her for a long moment. She was certainly attractive. If Karl Swenson had been prowling around, as

several people in town had told Frank he was, Karl could
have done much worse than prowl around out here.

"Then you know what happened to Karl?"

She sighed. A sadness touched her gaze. "Everybody
knows what happened to Karl."

"Any idea why he might do something like that?"

"After all these months you want to talk about it?"

"His widow, she—"

Liz Conway's gaze fell momentarily. She looked embarrassed at the mention of Swenson's wife.

Frank glanced around the cabin. There was a crude wood-
en sink, two wide cupboards, a double bed, a bookcase
filled with dusty volumes, and a rocking chair sitting empty
next to a window. On one long table running along the east
wall was a coffee mill, a fluting iron for putting ruffles in
calico, and several small red tins of Morey's brand spices,
everything from poultry seasoning to white pepper.

"You know his widow?" the woman asked.

"I don't. My brother does."

"I see. Then you were a family friend?"

Frank shrugged. "I knew Karl some. Not as well as my
brother knew him, though."

"Your last name Adams?"

"Right."

She brightened. "Karl used to talk about your brother all
the time. He was always planning to get in touch with him
again. I'm not sure he ever did."

"I think his missus stayed in touch with David. I don't
think Karl himself did." He hesitated. "I'm sure my questions are going to be hard for you."

She offered a quick, sad smile. "You're wondering if
Karl and I were lovers. Yes, we were. And you're wondering if I have any idea why he'd do such a terrible thing
to himself. No, I don't."

"You see him around the time he killed himself?"

"Not as often as I once had." She rolled her glass on its edge back and forth across the table. "He found other pleasures."

"Oh?"

She looked up at him. She didn't look happy. "You know a woman named Myra Livermore?"

"Guess I don't."

"She runs a house."

"A house?"

"You know, a cathouse." She stopped rolling her glass. "Anyway, he started going there."

Frank couldn't imagine giving up this woman as a mistress for a whore. But he kept his thoughts private.

"He stopped coming out here except when he was real drunk. And then he was too drunk to—well, you know. So we sort of became—friends—I guess. He told me things. You know, the way you'd tell a friend things."

"What sort of things?"

"Well, he told me all about Myra's for one thing. At first it all seemed to sort of amuse him. Karl never had a pot to pee in when he was a kid—he was a hardscrabble farmboy, in case you forgot—and his success went to his head. I kept thinking it was something else—you know, that he really wasn't just this hayseed who'd gotten lucky—but that's what it was. And then something happened at Myra's, and he changed."

"You have any idea what happened?"

She shook her head, her lustrous dark hair touching her shoulders. "No. Just something bad."

"Why do you say that?"

"Because of the way he'd act. Very guilty. When he'd come around, he'd ask for liquor, and then he just sit at this table here and brood." She frowned. "My husband was like

that when he drank, too. Wouldn't say much. Just kind of
kept to himself. But you could see there were things that
bothered him. One time I woke up in the middle of the
night, and I saw him sitting here crying. The way a man
cries, I mean. Almost like he doesn't know how." She
touched the tips of long fingers together and stared down
at them. "He was on a telegraph crew so he was gone a
lot. Worked as far away as Skagway. Maybe I just didn't
have the time to know him before he died."

"What killed him?"

She shrugged. "Heart attack. He was thirty-two years old.
Just fell dead."

Behind her beauty now, Frank saw weariness. He liked
her, and he felt sorry for her.

"Did Karl ever mention the bank robbery?"

She looked up at him again with her frank blue eyes.
"No. And I thought that was kind of funny."

"How so?"

"Well, here the bank is the biggest part of Karl's life
without doubt, but when it was robbed, he barely mentioned it."

"Not at all?"

"Just that it had happened and just that he hoped they
caught the robbers real soon. But for some reason he didn't
get worked up about it. I kept expecting him to." She
pointed to the wine bottle. "You like some more?"

"No, thanks."

She smiled. "You may as well. Your reputation is ruined,
anyway."

"My reputation?"

"Sure, don't you know who I really am?" Her tone turned
bitter. "I'm the widow woman who supposedly woos all the
fine husbands and fathers of Kelly Bay out here and then
seduces them with her magical powers."

"That's what they say?"

"Maybe that's not what they say, but it's sure what they think." She paused and looked down at her fingers again. "Karl was the one and only married man I ever carried on with. I admit I shouldn't have done it. It was the wrong thing to do for sure. But it was right after my husband died, and I guess I just felt afraid." She shook her head. "I shouldn't have done it. But I'm not the evil widow woman they think I am. I'm really not."

"Tell me again about the man who broke in here."

She laughed. "Well, he made it impossible for me to sleep soundly ever again, I'll tell you that. Now I'll sleep with a .44 next to my bed, and if I get three hours worth without waking up, I'll be lucky. He spooked me, that's for sure."

"He just came in the middle of the night?"

"Yes."

"And he started throwing things around, like he was looking for something?"

"Oh, he was looking for something. No doubt about that."

"Did he strike you?"

"Several times. And after he'd slap me, he'd say, 'Where'd you put it, you bitch?' I was half-afraid he was going to rape me and then kill me."

"But he never said exactly what he was looking for?"

"No."

"And you haven't figured out yet what it might be?"

"Nope. Though God knows I've tried. I sit here and try to think of what the man could have been looking for. It couldn't have been anything to do with my husband. As I said, he worked on a telegraph crew, which pays pretty well, but nobody would ever go busting into your cabin because you had these huge piles of money."

"Maybe the man who broke in here was looking for something that Karl left here."

"That's the only thing I can think of. This man thought that Karl gave me something, and that I've got it here."

"You don't think Karl might have hidden something here without your knowing it?"

She smiled. "Look around. This is pretty much a bare-bones cabin. Not a lot of hiding places. And besides, I already thought of that. So I've been looking. Got down on my hands and knees and searched every inch of this cabin. And didn't find a thing other than some old choke traps I'd forgotten about." "Choke" traps were devices that helped catch mice and rattlesnakes. Or so they claimed. Most frontier people found that they rarely worked properly.

"So you didn't find anything he might have left behind?"

"Not a thing, I'm afraid."

"You think you'd recognize your prowler if you ever saw him again?"

"Maybe. But it was pretty dark."

Now Frank understood why she'd been shooting at him. "Guess I don't blame you for being afraid."

He stood up, stretched some, and then smiled down at the widow. "I'm in town at the Mountie cabin if you need to talk to me."

She stood up and touched his elbow. "Sorry about all the gunfire."

"Well, at least it makes sense now. I don't blame you for being spooked."

She walked him to the door and outside into the soft spring day again.

"I miss him, you know that? Karl, I mean. He was really a sweet man, deep down." Her jaw set and her eyes narrowed. "I just wish I could have helped him. I wish I could have figured out what happened at Myra Livermore's."

As he swung his leg up on his mount, Frank said, "That's the very next thing my brother and I will be looking into, I'm sure."

"Myra Livermore's place?"

He nodded.

"I enjoyed meeting you. And I'm sorry again about shooting at you. In case you hadn't noticed, I wasn't really trying to kill you."

Frank grinned. "Yeah, I did notice that, ma'am, and I'm most appreciative." He tightened the reins. "And if you remember anything else, I'd appreciate it if you'd come into town and tell me."

With that, he rode off.

chapter
fifteen

IN THE MIDDLE OF THE AFTERNOON, ROBINSON took the key from Myra's office and went up to the attic. Aside from Myra, he was the only person in the house ever allowed up there.

He climbed the stairs to the second and then the third floor and then made quick work of letting himself into the attic. When the girls heard him coming, they tended to peek out of their rooms to see if they could get of glimpse of what went on up there. They were just as curious as many of the customers about what happened beyond the dark brown door with the fat Yale lock.

There were straight steps at a sixty-degree angle. Robinson was always breathing heavily by the time he reached the top of them. The walls on either side of the steps were coffin-narrow, and this always spooked Robinson because he frequently had nightmares of being buried alive. This had happened to one of the women back on the plantation, and she'd literally been driven mad. After she scratched and clawed her way to live again, she was never the same, but spoke only of demons and foul sins.

Sometimes, as soon as he had opened the attic door and then locked it behind him, he heard the girl up there humming to herself. At these times, he always wondered if she had been driven mad, too. Who could hum so happily in such a circumstance?

Robinson coughed. The dust was bad in the attic. He had four steps to go. There was no humming now, no sound at all except a pigeon cooing outside on the roof. He sneezed; the attic was dusty as hell.

When he got up there, the girl was sitting on the edge of the big brass double bed. The sheets were red silk and the pillows were small and heart-shaped. The scent of perfume—which Myra liberally splashed everywhere, including on the girl—was almost overwhelming. It made Robinson sneeze again. As for the rest of the furnishings, there was a nice mahogany bureau, and a large mirror, again heart-shaped, that sat on a small dressing table to the right of the bed. In all, the furniture looked as if it were part of a stage set, just as the girl did not look quite like a girl at all, but rather an actress.

Robinson had given up trying to guess how old she was. Hell, the girl herself didn't know. She'd been raised on the streets of old Montreal, which were some of the roughest slums in the world thanks to the collapsing Canadian economy, and sometimes she thought she was thirteen and other times she thought she was fifteen.

Myra, of course, told the customers that the girl, Jane, was eleven years old. This appealed to a certain kind of man, a driven and dark kind of man, a man willing to pay for a certain kind of sex that he did not want anybody else to know about.

So Jane, if that was in fact her name, was carefully made up to look like a little girl, her blonde hair always in ringlets, her dresses always ruffled, her stockings always loose on her thin little legs. She was one of those young girls who always seem younger anyway, with a kind of naive way of talking, a vulnerable way of looking at you, as if she's afraid. She was no more than five-feet tall, and Robinson would have been surprised if she weighed eighty pounds.

The chain was the final, theatrical touch, and it was a good one. No faulting Myra there. She was a stage magician of sorts—she knew how to cast a seductively evil atmosphere over everything.

A long, jangling silver chain had been locked to Jane's ankle and nailed with formidable spikes to the floor. Jane could never move more than seven feet from the bed, and when she did move, she sounded like Marley's ghost, the sound of the thick, rattling chain evil in the dark, dusty air of the attic.

Jane sat on the edge of the bed now, humming the same old song to herself, watching Robinson climb the stairs.

"Hi, Robinson."

"Afternoon, Jane."

"You're late today."

"Had some business."

"You come up here to take me away?"

He looked at her. "You sure are a child with a one track mind."

"You would be, too, if you had a chain around your ankle."

Thinking back to the plantation, he said, "Honey, I did have a chain on my ankle for a time."

"Really and truly?"

"Really and truly."

"I'm glad you got away, Robinson."

"So am I, child, so am I."

Robinson did his work first, which was cleaning the attic. He swept the floor, he emptied the cuspidor and the ashtray, he changed the sheets.

Then he told her to step over to the basin on the bureau and give herself a bath. Just before she did this, he poured fresh water from a porcelain pitcher into the bowl.

He never watched her bathe.

He went halfway down the stairs and sat there on the other side of the wall so that she couldn't see him and he couldn't see her. He wanted her to know that he wasn't like the others. He wanted her to know that he felt nothing but love and respect for children. He wanted her to know that she could trust him.

She hummed as she bathed, her voice sweet and girlish on the afternoon air.

When she was finished, she said, "You can come up now, Robinson."

And so he did.

She'd changed clothes, or at least colors. Myra had bought eight outfits for Jane. They were all pretty much the same— all fastidiously designed to make Jane look crushingly young and vulnerable—so Jane always giggled that she wasn't really changing clothes, she was just changing colors.

Robinson sat on the bed with her.

He said it simply. He saw no reason to tease her. "You know how we talk about you and I going away?"

She nodded, looking at him with her big sad eyes.

"Well, that's going to happen very soon."

"It is?"

"Yes. I'll be coming into some money very soon." He thought of the bridge and what lay beneath it.

"Where will we go?"

"America."

"Really and truly?"

He laughed. "Really and truly."

"How will you get the chain off me?"

"I think I know where she keeps the key."

She touched his arm. "I hope it's soon, Robinson. She—came up again last night."

He thought of what Myra probably did to this girl. He felt pure rage. "I'm sorry, Jane. It won't be long now."

"You promise?"

"I promise."

And then she was in his arms, and crying softly, the way she did sometimes. He just held her. He didn't know what else to do.

He hoped the key to the chain was where he thought, and he hoped the money beneath the bridge was where he thought.

"It won't be long, Jane."

"I'm scared, Robinson," she said. "Myra always says she'll kill me before she lets me go."

"I'll handle Myra. Don't you worry."

"You really think you can handle Myra, Robinson?"

He felt a fist forming. He did not hold with hitting women, but then Myra barely qualified as a woman. Especially given the way she used this little girl.

"You let me do all the worrying, child. You hear?"

He kissed her chastely on the forehead, then picked up her dirty clothes and the water she'd used to bathe herself, said goodbye, and went downstairs.

Somewhere on the second floor, he heard Myra's sharp, lecherous laugh. She was in one of the rooms with one of the girls. He thought to himself, Yessir, Miss Myra, you get a lot more pussy than any man I know. But you're not going to be bothering Jane much more.

Not much more at all.

chapter
sixteen

AFTER ROBINSON LEFT, THE GIRL WENT BACK
to her bed, the chain making a harsh noise as she dragged
it across the wooden floor. She lay for a time with her
eyes closed, trying to form a perfect dream to escape
into.

Sometimes she imagined herself a princess. She was
sixteen years old and quite beautiful and lived in a golden
castle by a deep blue stream. She was visited frequently by
a knight on a white steed. She had never seen the knight
because he was hidden beneath his helmet and armor, but
she knew he was handsome. And she also knew he was
good because he had slain an ugly dragon for her.

*Hey, little bitch, you know what I want, the man had
said to her on that first night that Myra had brought her
to the attic.*

*The man had only one eye, the other concealed beyond
a black eye-patch. He was unshaved, and his breath was
so foul, it stunned her. She thought that he must be at least
sixty or seventy years old, the way he moved so slowly and
carefully. But then she realized that it was just because he
was drunk.*

*He didn't give her time to take her clothes off. He ripped
them off. And then threw her down on the bed. And then he
couldn't do anything. And the more he felt humiliated by*

his inability to perform, the angrier and meaner he got.

At one point he grabbed the steel band around her ankle and jerked it so hard that it cut into her flesh and started bleeding. He'd slapped her then, once, twice, three times, somehow holding her responsible for his own shortcomings.

For many months, before Robinson befriended her, the girl's only escape was her fantasy life.

One day she'd be a princess. The next day she'd be a rich American girl riding thoroughbred horses on a vast estate. Sometimes she'd be a stage star, a song-and-dance girl who could move audiences to great laughter and even greater sorrow, taking her bows and being deluged with sweet red roses tossed from the audience.

One night a man had played Russian roulette with her. It was clear that his enjoyment derived not from sex but from terrifying her.

He had a six-shooter and he took all the bullets out. She counted them—one through six—lying on her bed.

Then he ordered her to pick one of them up. She did so, handing it to him. He put the lone bullet into the chamber and then spun the cylinder.

"You know which one it's in?"

She shook her head.

He laughed. "Neither do I."

Then he started clicking the trigger. After the second one, she screamed. The man slapped her. Then he pulled the trigger again.

By this time, Myra had come thundering up the stairs. The girl was Myra's prize. She didn't want anybody to spoil that prize. The girl had never seen a woman beat a man the way Myra had that night. She slapped and kicked him until his face was nothing but blood, then she pushed him down the stairs. The man, slamming his head against the wall, screamed all the way down.

It was much nicer to dream of white knights galloping across a meadow. Much nicer to hear the music of lutes. Much nicer to smell a lovely summer day by a lovely summer brook. And so the girl dreamed . . .

After a time, she woke up. She felt her usual disappointment on waking: she was not a princess, this was not a castle, and a white knight was not about to rescue her. Then she thought of Robinson.

Maybe not a white knight but how about a black knight? Yes, her very own black knight, and his name was Robinson. He had promised to show her a better life, to take her away from the attic and the clutches of Myra.

Soon, she hoped. Soon, she prayed. She closed her eyes again. She just hoped Robinson was telling her the truth.

Robinson was the only friend she had in the entire world, and if something ever happened to him . . .

She said a prayer now. Please, God, be with Robinson. Help him. And help me. Please, Lord.

Then she closed her eyes again. It was fun to be a princess.

chapter
seventeen

THERE WERE MANY MEN IN THE PROVINCES LIKE
Gatineau, a third generation trapper and hunter who had
tired of the wilds and come to town to do odd jobs, legal
ones when possible, illegal ones if necessary. He was virtually fearless, having fought wolf and bear with nothing
more than a knife and having survived six mining towns
where murder seemed to be mandatory.

He had come to Kelly Bay two years ago, lived in a
street hotel, where he slept on the floor near a large stove
and bathed in the river and shaved with his Bowie knife. He
had a thrice-busted nose, only a few teeth, and a big gouge
in the top of his left ear. While he'd eventually managed to
kill the bear that had attacked him, the struggle had been
a close one. As for age, he wasn't sure. The way he was
raised, there was little time or inclination to such niceties.
He was most likely around forty years old.

He stood in the vestibule of Myra Livermore's house,
hoping for a glimpse of the girls. He worked for Myra
whenever he was summoned. Unfortunately, she had a
strict rule that he was to leave the girls alone. She wouldn't
even let him pay for them. She said, quite bluntly, that there
were other houses in Kelly Bay more suitable for a man like
him, and that he should go there when his needs became
overwhelming.

Late afternoon sunlight beamed through the stained glass of the front door, painting the parquet floor in the vestibule the color of blood.

"In here."

Myra had put her head out of her office and waved him down the hall. He wouldn't see the girls, after all.

Myra's office was neat as always, reminding him, with its roll-top desk and its leather furniture, of a regular business office. The cigar Myra was smoking didn't hurt the business office image, either. She sat in a swivel chair with her feet up on her desk, fancy high-topped shoes laced all the way up, holding her cigar out in front of her as if admiring the color of the tobacco and the scent of the smoke.

He came in, feeling embarrassed about being in a place this fine, knowing he didn't belong in such fine trappings.

"You put that paper down."

"Yes, ma'am."

He leaned over and picked up a sheet of newspaper and set it on one of the cushions of the couch. She always made him sit on the paper, not wanting to dirty or discolor the leather. He sat down.

"I'm going to need you tonight."

"All right, ma'am."

"I'm going to pay you double what I regularly do."

Gatineau had two reactions to this: one, he was glad that his usual fee would be doubled. Two, he was wary of what she had in mind. Gatineau was strictly a small-time crook, with no aspirations to be anything more. He had no desire for the wrath of the Mounties or the cold reality of prison.

Plus, he always thought of what had happened in Dawson that time when he'd been been involved in an armed robbery. It had been years ago now, but the memory was vivid. It was supposed to be neat and simple and clean, but the proprietor of the little store had made a remark about

Gatineau's parentage, about what human dung people like Gatineau really were, the sons of trappers not being held in high esteem by townfolks, reeking as they did of dead animals and blood.

And something had happened to Gatineau right then. He'd backhanded the man so hard that the man flew across the room. Gatineau didn't stop there. He started kicking the man, first in the ribs, then in the chest, then in the face. The man pleaded for mercy, but it was as if Gatineau didn't hear him. He just kept kicking the man until the little Irish bastard had folded up double and lay in an unmoving heap behind the counter. The other thief had tried to stop Gatineau, but it had done no good. He went right on until the Irishman was very near dead.

Gatineau had never forgotten that night. In frontier Canada, you could survive as a petty crook, eluding the redcoats, if you kept all your jobs small, but once you attracted their attention, prison and maybe even the gallows was certain to be your fate.

Now, given what Myra had said about paying him double, his stomach started to knot, and he remembered the little Irish bastard. An image of the gallows came to him—of a man dangling neck-broken from the end of a noose and fouling himself so that the crowd below turned away in disgust. Gatineau had seen hangings. He knew what they were like.

"What's the job, ma'am?"

"I need to get some information from somebody."

"Like when you had me go to Liz Conway's last night?"

"Exactly." Myra took a long drag on her cigar and then raised her eyes to him. "This is a little different."

"How so, ma'am?"

"There's a woman, just like before, but there's also two little girls."

Then Gatineau knew why she was going to pay him

double. When children were in the picture, things got very serious indeed. It was an easy step up the gallows.

"I don't do things like that, ma'am."

"Nobody would have to get hurt. You'd just have to scare them a little."

"Not children. I don't do anything that involves children."

Myra took another drag on her cigarette. From upstairs came the sounds of her girls talking and laughing. Gatineau wondered what it would be like to have women that fine and that clean.

"You ever been to Quebec?"

"No, ma'am."

"You've heard about it?"

"Yes, ma'am."

"They've got everything there. Everything."

"Yes, ma'am."

"A man like you with money in his pocket, you could have yourself a real good time."

"Yes, ma'am." He saw what she was trying to do, of course. "But I just don't want anything to do with children."

She gaped over the top of her cigar. "That's where I'm going, Gatineau."

"Where?"

"Quebec."

"You're leaving Kelly Bay?"

"Soon as I find the money."

She had told him about the Kelly Bay bank robbery and how the loot was still somewhere around here.

"Then I'll be going on to Europe."

"What about the girls?"

She laughed. "Hell, man, they can take care of themselves."

She brought her feet down from the desk. She looked dead to him sometimes, like a corpse with too much makeup.

Especially when she smiled. Something terrible happened to her eyes when she smiled, a coldness that scared him a little.

She looked at him. "I'll go with you tonight. I'll make sure nothing happens to the two little girls."

"Then why would you need me to go?"

"Because I'll take care of the two little girls, and you could take care of the wife."

"You wouldn't hurt the girls?"

"Won't lay a hand on them," Myra said. "I'll just keep them upstairs while you get the widow to tell us where the money is. She's the last one left. We've tried everybody else. He had to tell somebody, and now I'm sure it was his wife."

"I don't know, Myra."

"Three times your usual price."

His head rose. So did his gaze. He looked at her. "Three times?"

"That's what I said. Three times, and a ticket to Quebec."

What she was outlining certainly had appeal, that he couldn't deny. If his dread was the gallows, his dream was of a clean-shaven good time in a big city. He'd never had that. Oh, he'd been in mining towns when a vein was struck, but that was different. The whores didn't get any better, the whiskey wasn't any purer, and the beds weren't any softer. There was just more gold dust.

"Three times, Gatineau. Think about that. For once in your life you'd actually have some real money in your pocket. And Quebec—"

"You really wouldn't hurt the children?"

"No."

"And I wouldn't have to hurt the lady?"

"No."

"And we could leave for Quebec—"

"Right away. Soon as we find out where the money is buried."

"It's tempting."

Myra leaned forward and smiled at him. As always, there was death in her eyes. She seemed to know the secrets of the grave. "Right now I'm going to let you go upstairs and take your pick of the girls."

"You serious?"

"I'm serious. They've just had their baths, and they're just gettin' ready for tonight—and you get your pick of them."

He thought of the girls he'd glimpsed in the windows of this house. Pretty ones and plump ones and tall ones and skinny ones, and every one of them good looking in her own particular way.

"How does that sound?" Myra said. She could see he was coming around.

"I just don't want them little girls to be hurt," he said.

"You don't have to worry about that."

"And we'll leave for Quebec as soon as we get the money?"

"The very same hour. I promise. We'll take a buckboard, and we'll ride to the depot thirty miles from here, and we'll get a train."

"I'm just worried about them little girls."

"It ain't the little girls you should be worryin' about," Myra laughed. She stood up and came over and pinched his cheek. "It's them girls upstairs you should be worryin' about. Which one of 'em you're going to pick for yourself?" She slid the cold slab of her hand into his. "Now, come on, Gatineau, let's get up there and get you a girl."

Reluctantly, he was pulled to his feet, and reluctantly, he followed her up the stairs.

He just kept thinking about those two little girls. Please, Lord, please don't let nothin' happen to those little girls, he thought. Please.

chapter
eighteen

THERE HAD BEEN A TIME WHEN THE NUGGET RES-
taurant had been much more boisterous than tonight. Back
in the days when Kelly Bay's first few gold strikes had
been announced, the restaurant had been packed with people of every kind—respectable town folks, rough miners,
filthy trappers, whores, cardsharps, and even an occasional
lawman and circuit preacher—all eating and drinking at the
largesse of the man who'd struck gold. The suddenly rich
man was invariably foolish with his money, spilling bags
of gold dust all over the bar, for example. The bartender,
who stayed sober to take advantage of the situation, would
get out a little dustpan and broom and sweep up the gold
dust. Many a bartender had gone home wealthy by the end
of such an evening.

And the place was loud with music, with the rich
miner hiring as many as a dozen musicians to play late
into the night. The whores worked the floor, of course,
steering their dancing partners to the bar at the end of
each dance so the partner could pay an exorbitant price
for a watery drink. There had even been gambling—faro,
keno, three-card poker, red dog, and roulette— and
with gambling came violence. God forbid you should
travel alone. If you did, somebody was bound to follow you out into the winter night, knock you unconscious,

and take whatever you had, be it pennies or sacks of gold.

There was the law, to be sure, but this was before the Mounties were of sufficient strength to have a regular post here, so lynching was not uncommon. Unfortunately, the lynch party often found in the morning that they'd strung up the wrong man, and then made a head-bowed pilgrimage to a cabin on the edge of town, there apologizing devoutly to the woman their drunken fury had made a widow. Then, of course, the crowd would feel so sorry for what they'd done that they'd head right back to the Nugget where they'd start drinking again.

Tonight, at the five o'clock dinner hour, there was neither a roulette wheel in sight, nor a miner, nor a lynch party, and about the strongest thing anybody seemed to be drinking was a beer or two. There was one waitress, a venerable white-haired lady who looked as if she'd start bawling if you said anything ornery to her, and a gigantic Eskimo who appeared to be the cook.

Frank wondered if the Eskimo was doing his own butchering in the back. The man's apron was a deep red. In the light, it even glistened with fresh blood. Frank thanked the Lord that he'd been gifted with a strong stomach.

Over coffee and David's pipe, the men had spent the past hour discussing what they'd learned today about Karl Swenson. Each man had interviewed three people. Each man had learned enough to know that a woman named Myra Livermore was probably going to be worth seeing.

"Something happened out there," David said.

"That's certainly the impression I got from Liz."

David smiled. "Liz, eh? You planning on seeing 'Liz' again by any chance?"

"Lonely widow woman. Hell, I'd only be doing my civic duty."

"Your civic duty," David said. "Uh-huh."

"I'd sure like to know who broke into her cabin and beat her up."

"I've got to admit, that's pretty interesting."

David looked out at the street. The lamps had been lit. Dusk was falling chill and quick. If you needed any reminder that summer wasn't here yet, all you had to do was feel the temperature drop to forty after dark.

"The thing I'm curious about is the robbery," David said.

"Then you're thinking the same thing I am."

David nodded. "Right. That maybe the robbery loot is still around here, and that's what everybody is trying to find. At least the man who broke into your friend Liz's cabin, anyway."

"Things don't sound so good for Karl, do they?"

David shook his head. "I'm afraid not. He was doing all sorts of things he shouldn't have."

"You'll have to ask Anna some more questions."

David nodded. "I'm not looking forward to it. When she hears the questions I'll have to ask her, she's never going to forgive me."

Frank sighed. "Well, why don't we go out to Myra Livermore's around seven?"

David laughed. "I thought we were going to go around nine. You must be getting pretty eager."

"It's strictly an official call."

"Right."

"Course," Frank said, "if one of those gals happened to knock me over the head and drag me upstairs, there really wouldn't be a lot I could do about that, now would there?"

"I guess not."

The men stood up and put their money on the table. They both left extra money. They didn't want the old white-haired lady with the exceptionally sad eyes to break into tears. They'd never be able to live with the guilt.

"Well, why don't I meet you at the Mountie post at about six-thirty, then?"

David nodded.

The men walked out to the boardwalk, took deep breaths of the clean, piney air, and then set about their separate tasks.

chapter nineteen

WHEN GATINEAU REACHED THE ROOMS UP-
stairs, he quickly forgot about the two little girls and the
danger that lay ahead tonight. As he followed Myra down
the narrow hall, he realized he was wide awake and walking
through a dream.

In every room, he saw half-naked women. In one room,
he saw a young woman at a mirror, brushing her long,
blonde hair. She was completely naked. His eyes took in
every curve and hollow of her young body. An overpowering lust took him over.

Myra had stopped. "You like that one?"

"Yes'm."

"You sure?"

"Yes, ma'am, I'm sure."

"She's got a sister, you know."

"She does?"

"Follow me."

Gatineau walked down to the end of the hall, to the final
room off the corridor.

"Take a peek in there," Myra said. Her eyes sparkled as
she pointed to the interior of the room. Clearly, she was
proud of her girls and loved showing them off.

Gatineau peered into the room. His smelly, ragged head
gave a small start as he saw that the same girl now stood in

this room before a mirror—only this girl wasn't blonde, she was dark-haired. The walls of the small room flickered with lamplight. The air smelled sweetly of perfume and sachet. There was a brass bed, the covers turned down, with blue frilly pillows fluffed up at the head of the bed. But Gatineau kept his eyes on the girl.

This one, like the other, was slight of frame and very pretty. Also like the other girl, she looked young, fifteen at the oldest. Curiously, however, where the other girl's smile had been knowing, even insinuating, this girl's smile was innocent.

"Identical twins," Myra smiled, "except for the hair."

Gatineau didn't know what to say. He felt dumber than usual, as if he'd been tricked as only a rube could be tricked. "They're really two different girls?"

"They really are." Myra laughed. "You think the blonde one ran down here real quick and put a wig on?"

Gatineau stared into the room. The girl was facing him now, her bush and small, upturned breasts showing him that she was way beyond modesty.

"How would you like 'em both?" Myra said.

"Both?"

"You'd have to pay a lot for both of 'em ordinarily, but seeings as how you're doing some work for me—" Myra shrugged.

"You serious?"

"I am."

"Both of 'em?"

She leaned in. "Both of 'em, Gatineau. But I want you to do just exactly what I tell you to tonight. You understand me?"

"Yes, ma'am."

By now, he had forgotten all about the two little girls and the prospect of prison or a noose. All he could think of were the two young whores. Imagine what it would be like rolling around in bed with both of them. Imagine what it would be like drinking beer some time, boasting of such a night to your drinking friends.

"We understand each other, Gatineau?"

"Yes, ma'am."

Myra smiled and clapped him on the shoulder. "Good. Now you go down to the end of the hall and wait. I'll call you in a few minutes. Both girls'll be in this room waiting for you."

Gatineau took one last look at the naked dark-haired girl smiling at him. Oh, my God, tonight was sure going to be special. It sure was.

He went down to the end of the hall and waited for Myra to call him back to the Eden he'd been temporarily banished from.

chapter
twenty

"I WANNA SAY GRACE TONIGHT, MOMMY," SIX-year-old Agnes said.

Sara said, "It's my turn, Mommy, isn't it?"

Anna Swenson couldn't help herself. "Girls, do you really think we should be arguing over who gets to say Grace? Don't you think that's a little disrespectful to the Lord?"

"What's dic-recpectable mean?" five-year-old Sara asked.

"Disrespectful means that we don't show people how much we care about them."

"But she said Grace last night, Mommy!" Agnes said.

"Huh-uh, Mommy!" insisted Sara.

Anna reached out, palms flat. Each girl put a tiny hand in hers. Anna closed her eyes and bowed her head. "Mommy will say Grace."

And so she did. As she prayed, fleeting memories of her husband came back to her. Christmas dinner. Gentle nights in bed. The birth of their children, with Karl standing by, cooling her head with a damp washcloth as the midwife worked feverishly to bring forth the infant. Regular family dinners, night after night, Anna believing that they would always have such dinners, that he would always be here.

And now this emptiness that the months had only deepened. The wisdom of her pastor, the wisdom of her friends in Kelly Bay, was that time would eventually heal her pain and loneliness. But she wanted to know *when*.

Then she felt ungrateful, felt that *she* was showing a lack of respect to the Lord. Didn't she have her two lovely daughters, their little heads bowed now in prayer, the soft lantern light playing off their soft, blonde hair? Didn't she have a sound roof over her head, and a little cash put aside, and friends she could call on when she needed company or advice?

She finished Grace, giving the girls' hands an extra, warm tug.

"Can I say it tomorrow night, Mommy?" Sara said, ever the persistent one.

Anna smiled. "We'll see. Now let's eat."

"Tomorrow night I get to say it," Agnes said, just as Anna took her first bite of homemade wheat bread.

It was going to be one of those nights. She decided she'd put the girls to bed early and get out the Louisa May Alcott novel she was reading. A night of escape into the world of *Little Women* sounded awfully good to her.

And then the panic was there, the inexplicable panic that she'd felt all day. Her eyes flitted from one window to another. She half-expected to see a face in one of the windows, a face peering ominously in.

Ever since waking this morning, she'd sensed that something terrible was going to happen today. At first, she'd put this feeling down to the general apprehension she'd known since her husband's terrible suicide. It seemed pretty natural that a widow with two daughters would sometimes get anxious about being alone.

But today, this seemed to be something more, something specific. As if some event, some horrible event, were going to take place today. She looked again at the windows, but saw nothing. Just the moonlit clouds racing past the half-moon.

She felt calmer, then, sitting here with her girls. She watched them eat, their heads bowed, their hair shining, both of them trying hard to honor the table manners she'd taken pains to teach them. And for the most part, they were very well-mannered little girls, but every once in a while, when she thought Anna might not be looking, Sara's hand would shoot out, and she'd grab something instead of using her fork. Ordinarily, Anna would say something, but not tonight.

Then she heard the shed door slam. She froze. The girls didn't hear the door but they did see their mother sit up bolt straight, fear playing across her pretty face.

"What's wrong, Mommy?" Agnes said.

"You girls keep eating," Anna said. "Mommy will be right back."

And with that, she got up from the table, dashed into the kitchen, and grabbed the railroad-style lantern Karl always preferred. It took three matches to light it properly, her hands were shaking that badly. Wrapping a shawl around herself, she went out the back door and started down the slope to the shed.

Since the night Karl killed himself, she rarely spent much time down here. It was simply too terrible a reminder of what had happened. It was no better for her tonight.

The shed itself was lost in deep shadows, its windows like the dead eyes of a blindman, the front door banging again and again against the frame, the sound stark and eerie in the night.

She forced herself to think of something else, anything but the sight of Karl's charred body that morning. Even though she'd sold Karl's horse right after the funeral, the shed still stank of pissy hay and horse manure. She closed the shed door tight, wrapping the latch with a length of dangling rope. Then she started back to the house, quickly, not wanting to leave the girls alone.

Midway between the shed and the house, clouds covered the moon, and in that moment of pitch darkness, Anna felt almost child-like—alone and terrified and filled with dread. Something awful awaited her tonight, she was sure of it. Uttering a silent prayer, she hurried inside to be with her daughters again.

chapter
twenty-one

THE EVENING CAME WAY TOO SOON FOR GAT-
ineau. He had helped himself to not merely one of Myra
Livermore's finest but two—a blonde and a dark-haired
wench. While they made it obvious that they wished he'd
taken a bath first, they finally got over their reservations
and began to work him over with quick expertise. At various points, he cried out, felt he was going blind, yelped, felt
pleasure and pain at the same time, and in general realized
all over again why the Good Lord had gone and created
women.

For nearly three hours, it was a world of soft flesh
and open mouths—in other words, one of the dreams he
had when he was out on his lonesome somewhere in the
woods where there were only Indian or buffalo trails of no
more than twelve-inches across. He'd lay awake for hours
taunting himself with erections and daydreams of just such
moments as these. And now they'd come true. Then came
the knock, Myra's sharp bullying knock, and he knew his
dream had ended.

He might have hoped that the two girls had looked a
little more distressed by the fact that all this was coming
to an end. Indeed, he caught one of them winking at the
other, as if they'd just shared a silent joke of some kind.
But he paid them no mind. He wanted to make this a

totally good experience. The girls drifted out of the room, giggling at each other, pushing past their boss Myra, and floating off down the hall, still giggling, the smart-mouth little bitches.

Gatineau got his clothes on.

Myra came into the room, looked around frowning and said, "We'll have to get this ready for tonight right away." She stuck her head out the hall and said, "Where the hell's that Rosarita when you need her, anyway?"

Rosarita said, "This lantern should do you."

Robinson took the unlighted lantern from the Mexican woman and nodded his thanks.

Robinson and Rosarita had long ago formed a friendship based on their mutual contempt for Myra Livermore, even though Robinson feared the Mexican woman's moods sometimes—she could seem almost insane at certain moments. So, though he liked her, he kept a safe distance from her.

But tonight when Robinson needed a shovel and a pick axe and a lantern, he went to Rosarita. She had a key to the storeroom, Robinson didn't. Myra kept most doors locked, and nobody but her had keys to all the rooms. Rosarita had the storeroom key because all the cleaning material was kept there.

The place was narrow, with damp, swollen plaster walls, low-hanging cobwebs, a mud floor and at least a half-dozen rats. Rosarita's own lantern was lighted and cast the room into deep, menacing shadows. Not even Robinson wanted to stay down here any longer than necessary, and given all the pain and travail of his life, there was little that Robinson truly feared.

A knock came on the door leading to the room.

"Yes?" Rosarita called up the stairs.

One of the whores yelled back, "Myra's looking for you."

"Tell her just a minute."

"She sounds like she's in a hurry."

Rosarita smiled to Robinson. "Bitch is always in a hurry. Except when she's working out on the bed with one of those whores of hers."

"Yeah, then she takes her time."

"She takes her time real good."

Rosarita sighed, hefted the lighted lantern, and nodded for Robinson to follow her upstairs.

After Rosarita appeared and started cleaning up the room, Myra and Gatineau went downstairs to her office.

She poured him a sizable drink of good whiskey, which he treated like so much rotgut by knocking it back immediately, and then he said, "You just remember, I done a lot of things in my life, but I ain't gonna hurt no kids."

"Not asking you to. I just want you to help me scare their mother by pretending you're gonna hurt them."

"What if she don't know where the money is?"

"Oh, she knows all right."

"How can you be sure?"

"Who else would he tell?"

Gatineau shrugged. "Maybe he didn't tell nobody."

"Oh, no. I knew Karl Swenson pretty good. And he was a talker. Liked to gab and liked to brag. This wasn't the sort of thing he would have kept to himself."

"How about one more drink?"

"You gonna show this one a little respect?"

"What's that supposed to mean?"

"It means why don't you savor the flavor a little bit instead of throwin' it down like you were in some kind of contest or something."

He shrugged. She was a strange old bitch, Myra was, and not just because she liked pussy, either. She was more

like a man than a woman, and that had always spooked
Gatineau.

"You gonna show it a little respect?"

"Yep. Yes indeed."

So she poured him another drink.

In five minutes, they left for Anna Swenson's house.

chapter
twenty-two

ROSARITA WAITED ON THE BASEMENT STEPS until she heard Myra and Gatineau leave. Tonight would be the night.

The time was right, and she had the courage.

Despite the fact that Rosarita gave the impression of being both slow and cowardly—she took endless amounts of brutal teasing from the whores—she was a woman with her own quiet kind of dignity. Tonight she planned to repay herself for all the years that she had toiled in this whorehouse.

Now, she opened the basement door and listened intently. The house was settling into the night's usual activities: the player piano was starting up, the girls were laughing, people plodded up and down the staircase.

Now would be a perfect time.

Rosarita moved from the shadows of the basement steps and came up into the kitchen which was, as usual, empty. She smelled spices and boiling meat. Grabbing a broom from the closet so she'd appear to be busy, Rosarita left the kitchen and started down the curving hallway toward Myra's office.

Earlier, she had thought of taking a gun from one of the girls—despite what Myra might think, the girls would someday probably rise in up in revolt, kill her, take her money, and flee—but then she decided that that would only add to the danger. She wanted to make a swift, clean run on Myra's office and get out of here—forever.

At the end of the hallway, two whores appeared, their arms around each other. They were already drunk. They looked at Rosarita and giggled.

"My, aren't you looking beautiful this evening?" one of them said.

The other winked at her friend. "And such a beautiful dress."

Rosarita hung her head. As the twelfth child of an itinerant Mexican stoop laborer, she did not have to be reminded that her looks had long since faded into ugliness. Of that there was no dispute.

The girls pushed past her, making sure that they knocked her painfully against the edge of the doorway. This was the treatment she usually got from the whores. She had suffered it for so long, but soon . . . .

Five minutes later, she stood in the darkness outside Myra's office. She had been unable to steal a key, but she had learned over the years how to pick virtually any lock with a piece of wire and a narrow length of metal. Perhaps she did not have looks or decent clothes, but let no man say that Rosarita did not have brains.

She looked both ways, bent over, and proceeded to pick the lock.

It was sweaty, terrifying work. Every few moments, Rosarita thought she heard something. Her head snapped up, her heart began to pound, and she felt a queasiness in both her stomach and her bowels.

She was not as brave as she thought.

But finally, it was done, and she pushed the door open and rushed inside. She stood in the shadows of the office, letting her heart find its normal rhythm, letting the icy sweat dry on her back and under her arms, letting her nose fill with the particular scents of this room—dead cigarette smoke, the wood shavings of freshly sharpened pencils, the faint aroma of Myra's oppressive perfume.

Now, the laughter and the music of the player piano seemed far away. For the first time, she felt safe.

She would take what she wanted, what she needed, what, after all the abuse both physical and mental, she deserved, then she would walk away to freedom.

She had taken two steps toward the massive roll-top desk, surely filled with goodies such as extra cash, when she heard footsteps in the hall outside and saw that she had left the door standing open an inch or two. She recognized the voice immediately. It belonged to the whore named Jody, the girl unofficially in charge when Myra was gone. Jody had won this honor because she was not only attractive—and spent many nights in Myra's private bed—but also because she was at least as mean as Myra.

"Who's in there?" Jody snapped.

Rosarita's body went through its turmoil again—freezing sweat, pounding heart, bowels threatening to burst and run down her legs. She froze.

Where could she possibly hide? And if she moved at all, wouldn't Jody hear her for sure?

"I said who's in there?" Jody said.

The irony was, as Rosarita sensed, Jody was afraid. If she had a gun, Jody would obviously have been bolder. It was clear the whore was now torn between opening the door and going back for a weapon.

"Jody? Jody?"

The girl's clear voice sailed down the narrow darkness of the hall as musically as a chord from the player piano.

"I'm busy," Jody said.

"Trouble upstairs. That man in the top hat? He just slugged Maizie."

"Sonofabitch," Jody said.

"You really better get up there. It's gettin' pretty bad."

Rosarita stood absolutely still, listening. What would Jody do?

Holy Mary Mother of God, Rosarita prayed. Please be with me.

And then Jody stepped forward, grasped the doorknob in her hand, and yanked the door shut. It closed with the finality of a coffin being sealed for all eternity.

Rosarita did not know how to respond. Was this good, what Jody had done, or would it only make Rosarita's problems worse?

Rosarita decided, for once, to look at a situation optimistically. Jody would go upstairs to tend to the trouble, leaving Rosarita to find herself money and perhaps even gold, and then when Rosarita had filled her pockets, all she had to do was take the wire and the piece of metal and sneak out.

Then Jody, on the other side of the locked door, said, "You stand here and watch the door."

"Watch the door?" the other whore said.

"Just make sure that nobody comes out of there."

"Gosh, Jody, I wish I knew what you were talking about."

"You just do what I say. Stand here and watch this door. I'll be back in a few minutes. You understand me?"

"If you say so," the other whore said sardonically.

Then there were the sounds of Jody walking away. Going down the hall. And then up the staircase.

Rosarita still stood there, frozen. This girl that was left in charge, Rosarita felt certain that she would have no trouble with her if it came to sneaking out and pushing past her, but for now all Rosarita could do was hide. If she started searching desk drawers for cash, the girl would hear her and likely go get a gun.

All Rosarita could do was tiptoe over to the closet, open the door, and hide inside. She would just have to wait to see what opportunity presented itself. Or wait for Jody to come back with a gun, find her in the closet, and kill her. She knew Jody pretty well, and Jody would take a deep and abiding pleasure in killing her. For sure.

chapter
twenty-three

SHE HAD HER FEARS AND PREJUDICES: SHE DIDN'T like snakes, and she didn't like Indians. She thought both should be killed summarily. She had these particular prejudices because she'd grown up on the Cree River, where battles with snakes and Indians were common and frequently deadly to the Irish immigrants who were her own.

As a girl, she'd baked thirty loaves of bread a week for her family of nine brothers and eight sisters. Because she was good at sewing, she was responsible for handknitting socks for the entire family, two pairs for each member. Her only amusement—escape, really—was going over in the wagon to the German community on Sundays after mass. The Germans were the wealthiest of all the Canadian immigrant groups on this part of the Cree and had brought many fine things with them, including thin china plates, gold-rimmed cups, mahogany and rosewood furniture, and real pianos.

Liz Conway thought of all these things as she sat in her cabin, comfortable in her rocking chair. The events of the day had left her exhausted, especially her brief gun battle with the U.S. Marshal Frank Adams, a man she liked more than she wanted to admit to herself. Which was why she was thinking about her girlhood—easier to forget Frank that way.

Eventually, thoughts of her girlhood fading, she started recalling her days as Karl Swenson's lover, all his late-night trips out here, and then the curious final months of their relationship when he'd been more like her brother than her lover. What had he been doing at Myra Livermore's that made him so ashamed? Certainly, just seeing a whore would not have caused such shame in him. And why had he been so mute on the subject of the bank robbery? Any time she brought up the subject, he changed the topic quickly, as if he were afraid to even discuss it.

Frank Adams's visit today had made her curious all over again. What could possibly have driven Karl Swenson to pour kerosene all over himself and then set himself afire?

Then, helpless to do otherwise, exhaustion claimed her, and she dozed.

Liz woke up half an hour later. In the cabin windows, full night had taken the sky. Even in here, she could tell it was too chilly to quite be summer yet. And then she thought of it; it came unbidden, but the moment she thought of it she realized that she should have told Adams about it this afternoon.

One night Karl had come out here particularly drunk. He'd thrown furniture around, he'd gone outside to throw up, he'd lain on the bed and made fists and fought back tears. Yet, at first, he wouldn't say a word, wouldn't offer her a clue about what was going on.

And then he said it. Three times in a period of five minutes, in fact. Said it with force and belligerence. "The bridge. The hell with 'em. They'll never find it. Not there."

She had dismissed it all as just more of his ravings. He wasn't a good drunk. He frequently got sick and crazy. Even more frequently, he ranted, repeating the same thing over and over.

But in light of Adams's visit this afternoon, she wondered if Karl's reference to a bridge might not have some bearing on Adams's investigation. She started to sit up in the rocking chair and then stopped. She was awfully tired. Wasn't this something that could wait until the morning?

She thought of the dark, lonely dirt road into town, and of the dropping temperature. She was ready for bed, not ready for a nocturnal ride. She sank back in the chair and closed her eyes.

She spent the next few minutes thinking of her girlhood again, of Christmas Eves round the fireplace, all the year's hard work seeming to be worth it in those warm, family moments. Unlike most immigrant families, hers had not stayed close. They had scattered everywhere and . . .

Actually, she wouldn't mind putting on her best shirt and her sheep-lined jacket and seeing Frank Adams again, she thought. Maybe he'd be so grateful for her information about the bridge that he'd invite her to supper one of these nights. She sat up in the chair, put her hands down on the arms, and pushed herself upward.

She hated to think of the day when the family curse, arthritis, invaded her joints and bones and made even a simple act like this one difficult and painful.

She got up on her feet, went over to the wash basin, and began getting herself ready for the twenty-minute ride into town. Here I come, Mr. Marshal, she thought, ready or not.

chapter
twenty-four

MYRA AND GATINEAU HAD JUST REACHED THE brothel's livery stable when they saw a Mountie and another man coming walking toward them. They appeared to have come out of nowhere, part of the shadows wavering under the moon.

"Evening, ma'am," the Mountie said, all spit and polish and politeness.

"Evening," Myra said. "Can I help you with something?"

"I'd like to talk to you for a few minutes, if you're Myra Livermore."

"I'm Myra Livermore but I'm afraid I'm in a hurry."

The Mountie touched the edge of his campaign hat with his gloved hand. "As I say, ma'am, it wouldn't take but a minute."

Myra said, "I have an agreement with the local officials."

"I don't doubt that, ma'am. That's not why I'm here."

Myra nodded to the burly man next to him. "Who's he?"

"Excuse me, ma'am, I should have introduced myself," the Mountie said. "I'm David Adams with the RCMP, and this is my brother, Frank. He's a U.S. Marshal."

"One blond, one dark-haired," Myra smiled. "And both good-looking."

David smiled back wryly.

Myra glanced at Gatineau. "You go ahead and get the buggy ready. I'll be back in a little bit."

The house was bright, clean, and smelled of perfume, tobacco smoke, and whiskey. The girls the Adams brothers saw were certainly not typical of whorehouses in this part of the provinces. They were not only clean, they were actually very pretty, all got up in frilly dresses and citified hairstyles.

Myra led them through down the hallway to a small parlor that had in the corner a desk, a filing cabinet, and a swivel business chair. Her regular office was down the hall, but she would not let lawmen in there.

Myra took off her wrap. She offered them bourbon and cigars; they declined both.

Myra sat down at the desk facing them, then she said, "All right, gentlemen, tell me why you're here."

"Karl Swenson," Frank said.

Myra's face tightened immediately. It was obvious that the name was not only familiar to her, but that it carried some kind of personal significance.

"Yes," she said, "I remember him." She was trying to sound impersonal, but her face had betrayed her.

"I understand he used to be a customer of yours," Frank said.

"We don't call them customers. We call them clients."

Frank smiled at the fancy labeling. "All right. I understand he was a client of yours."

"Yes, he was."

"Frequent client?" David asked.

"I guess that would be fair to say. Yes, frequent client."

"Did you know him well?" David said.

"Reasonably well, I suppose."

"Did he ever talk to you about his troubles?" Frank said.

"Not that I can remember."

"How about the robbery?" David said. "Did he talk about that, his bank being robbed?"

It was clear that Myra was doing her best to seem indifferent to this conversation, but she wasn't having much luck. She looked concerned and even vaguely angry.

"No, he never mentioned it."

"Did you ever think he'd kill himself the way he did?" David asked.

She shrugged. "Men do funny things sometimes."

David leaned forward. "What were his habits when he was here?"

"His habits?"

"You know, were his sexual tastes pretty normal?"

She hesitated before she spoke. " 'Normal' covers a lot of territory in a place like this."

Frank said, "Did he ever go in for rough sex?"

"Not that I know of."

"Or sex with men?"

She smiled. "Not Karl. Karl was strictly after women."

David said, "Do you have any 'special' rooms here?"

"Special?" she said, trying to sound naïve. But for somebody as battle-weary as Myra, sounding naïve was impossible. "I guess I don't know what you mean."

"Sometimes," Frank said, "places like this have a room that only preferred customers get to use."

"Customers with special tastes," David said.

"Young girls," Frank said.

"Very young girls," David said.

"The kind of girls women like you can get into trouble for," Frank said.

"Sometimes people who run houses like these find very young girls—usually runaways and usually scared—and the people who run the houses pretend to be their friend. They don't tell the young girls what they'll have to do to earn their board. Not until it's too late, anyway, when the young girls have already had to give themselves to older men."

"Nothing like that goes on here," Myra said. "I wouldn't stand for it."

David glanced at Frank.

Frank said, "He never talked about the robbery?"

"You asked me that once." She was nervous again.

"And you said no," Frank said.

"And that's still what I say. No. N-O. He never mentioned anything about it, and I didn't ask."

"Was he here the night he killed himself?" David said.

"I don't think so. I didn't see him, anyway."

"And you never had any hint that he might do something like this to himself?"

"Not a hint."

The men again exchanged glances.

David started tugging on his long gloves and then stood up. He put out a hand. Myra took it with a muscular grip. They shook.

"That's it?" Myra said.

"That's it," David said.

The relief on her face was almost pathetic.

From down the hall, the player piano exploded into a happy tune. There was laughter, glasses clinking. The festivities must have officially begun.

Myra escorted the two men out the door and down the hall.

"I wish I could have been more help," Myra said.

Frank winked at David.

David said, "You wouldn't even speculate on why he might have killed himself that way?"

She shrugged. "Like I said, men do strange things. Plus he was a brooder."

"I see."

"Liquor affects men differently. Some men get happy, some men miserable. Men with secrets, men with fears, those are the men it makes miserable. And that's how Karl was when he drank—miserable."

At the front door, a buxom young woman was talking to a very respectable-looking white-haired gentleman all natted up in a dark suit and a bowler. The buxom young woman had her hand on his crotch and was stroking him. The white-haired gentleman was grinning so ardently, he looked twenty years younger than he probably was.

The Adams brothers said good night to Myra and stepped out into the night. As they headed back toward the Mountie post, Frank said, "It does a man good to run into a sweet grandmotherly type like Myra every so often."

"You mean you think that the nice little old lady spoke with a forked tongue, brother?"

Frank's laugh was sharp as a gunshot in the chilly darkness. "Yeah, I'd say she spoke with a forked tongue, all right."

chapter
twenty-five

SHE COULD HEAR THEM DOWNSTAIRS. SHE COULD hear their beery jokes and their coarse laughter and their inane bragging. She was on the bed, lying face down, which was not easy given the limited access the chain gave her. She had her eyes closed, and she covered her ears with the flat of her palms.

She did not want to hear them. She did not want to see them. She wanted them to be dead.

The funny thing was, the girl had always heard tales about being kidnapped or shanghied or whatever you called it, but she always figured, in her hard, street-urchin way, that these were tales the nuns thought up, or the dour people at the Salvation Army thought up, or the policemen in their dusty uniforms thought up to scare young girls into going with the nuns or the soup-kitchen folks.

But then, by God, she'd actually been shanghied. She'd actually been pressed into slavery. And so here she was now.

In the dark attic, spindly branches scraped against the window, the moon rose wanly in a cobwebbed corner of the most distant pane, and the vague scent of kitty shit hung in the air.

Robinson had snuck her up a kitty for company one day—and how the girl loved it. She nearly suffocated the sweet little thing, holding it so tight, sleeping with it like it was a baby sister.

"You don't let that old bitch catch you with it, though," Robinson had warned. "She don't want you to have nothing she didn't bring you herself."

And Robinson's warning had come true.

The girl always successfully hid the kitty whenever Myra came up to the attic. Or she thought she hid her well, anyway.

But then one day Myra came up all flushed and wild-eyed, the way she seemed to get whenever one of the girls had sassed her back, and she said, "I want that thing."

"What thing?"

"You know good and well what thing. That cat."

"I ain't got no cat."

"The hell," Myra said.

And then she started searching the attic. The girl couldn't stop her because the chain wouldn't reach that far. All she could do was crouch in the corner, biting her tiny child-like fingers and saying, "Hail Mary full of grace, Hail Mary full of grace," so fast and so many times that after a while the words didn't even make any sense.

"Please don't hurt her," the girl started saying then, dropping all pretense that she didn't have a kitty.

Then Myra found her hiding under a blanket, seeming to know that there was a terrible enemy stalking her. Myra picked up the kitty savagely by the head and then carried it over to the girl.

"You remember what I told you about not havin' any secrets from me?"

"Yes, ma'am."

"Well, you should have told me about this here cat."

"Yes, ma'am. I'm sorry. If you let me keep her, I promise that I—"

"Keep her?" Myra said. "Keep her? After you went and lied to me this way?"

Then Myra did it. Right in the plain afternoon sunlight, right in front of the girl, no more than four feet away from her.

The girl had always suspected that Myra was strong. But not like this. Nobody should be this strong.

Myra held the small kitten's body in her left hand and then enveloped the kitten's head with her right. The kitten cried in great pain.

The girl clamped her hands over her ears, saying "Please don't hurt her, Myra. Please don't hurt her."

Then Myra, with seemingly no fuss at all, ripped the kitten's head from its body. She tossed the head, the eyes still open and staring, like a baseball against the wall.

The head left a trail of blood and brains as it slid down the wall to the floor.

"You ever gonna have secrets from me again, you little bitch?" Myra spat.

But the girl was sobbing too hard to say anything.

Myra smiled and left.

Yes, the stories were true. Young runaway girls did get kidnapped, did get sold into slavery, did have to spread their stick-like little legs so whiskey-breathed men could put their hot sex inside them.

She lay on the bed, eyes still closed, ears still covered, and dreamed of a time when she'd be free again. She missed the kitty so much. She still had nightmares about what Myra had done to it.

The wind came up again in the darkness. The silver moonlight was the only faint light in the attic. The branches scraped the window.

All the girl could do was wait and hope that Robinson

hadn't been lying to her today. He said he was going to help her get away. He'd promised, his sacred word. All the girl could do was pray that Robinson was able to do what he said he would.

chapter
twenty-six

THE DIGGING TOOK LONGER THAN HE THOUGHT it would. For one thing, there was the traffic, human traffic and wagon traffic alike. Robinson had had no idea how well the bridge spanning the two ends of Kelly Bay was traveled at night.

For another thing, there was his natural fear. As one of the few black residents of Kelly Bay, virtually everything Robinson did was suspicious to somebody. Any time there was a burglary, any time there was a woman molested, Robinson was suspected. During the day they didn't bother him so much—he was just a dumb old Negro, and they could see what he was doing—but at night they got nervous about having him moving around in the darkness.

So he had stood for a long time on the bluff overlooking the bridge, watching the dark shapes of the coaches cross the steel-and-concrete span, the horses nickering in the darkness, the passengers speaking in snatches of conversation ultimately lost to the night and the wind. It was cold as November on the bluff, and the lights of the Bay, the snug houses, the lights of the business district, made him feel lonelier than ever.

Finally, he came down the hill, walked beneath the bridge and set to work.

Somewhere below him, the water lapped icily on the shore. The lights of a barge could be seen hugging the opposite shore as it headed downstream to a furrier loaded with piles of bloody animal skins. A gaunt-ribbed dog prowled the rocky coastline hungrily. It paused for a frantic moment to gaze upslope at the figure of Robinson bent over the lantern, the knife-sharp edge of the shovel unearthing small piles of hard, cold dirt.

The actual shoveling went smoothly. What took a long time was pausing every few minutes when he thought he heard somebody coming.

A wagon seeming to stop on the bridge. A shadow seeming to come down the hill to his right.

The sense that somebody was sitting in the pavillion far to his left, watching him. Then he'd get back to work, dismissing his fears as foolish.

He kept thinking of the girl. This money would buy freedom for two people. He'd always wanted a child, and she was going to be that child for him. While there was still time, he wanted to show her that life could be good and clean and honorable, and that no matter how people tried to destroy you with their fears and envy and hatred, you could survive with your resolve and your dignity intact. It was not easy—life was never easy for people like Robinson or the girl—but it could be mastered if you tried hard enough. It was important to Robinson that the girl understand that.

And so he shoveled. And paused every few minutes to make sure that nobody was going to try and take advantage of what he was doing. He was through with people taking advantage.

In all, the shoveling took eighteen minutes. When he was finished, Robinson had two things: a formidable pile of dirt around a formidable hole, and a heavy satchel with the bank's name stenciled in black on the side. The satchel was damp and cold from being in the earth. Robinson tried not to think about how damp and cold a human body would get in the same dirt.

His long black fingers unclasped the satchel, and his strong black hand pushed deep into its depths. His sad brown eyes lighted with glee when the black hand returned with a handful of greenbacks.

The satchel was heavy, veritably pregnant, with money.

Robinson felt the foolish impulse to do a little dance. The last time he'd been this happy was seeing his youngest brother in St. Louis thirty-some years ago.

But Robinson was not a careless man. He knew that he needed to fill the hole back in, douse the lantern light and get away from here as soon as possible. He wanted to get back to Myra's. He had a plan for spiriting the girl away tonight. Myra would never get her dirty hands on the girl again.

Standing with the cold wind beginning to chafe, the satchel of money at his feet, the faint light in the lantern smudgy behind the streaky glass, Robinson made a promise to the girl. She'll never touch you again, Jane. I promise. I solemnly promise.

Robinson got to work. In five minutes, he'd bundled everything up and was moving quickly across the bridge, one shadow among many shadows in the night.

chapter
twenty-seven

THEIR FATHER HAD BEEN A TIRELESS READER, and he loved retelling what he'd read to the girls. Anna and the daughters would sit on the couch in the flickering light of the fancy banquet lamp with its onyx porcelain column and rose silk shade that cast a warm color through the living room.

How the girls loved to hear about the exploits of the mountain men and how they settled the province, holding off Indians and bears and whiskeyrunners in the process. They also loved the stories he told about the Mounties, especially after they'd pestered him to put on the red coat he'd worn when he'd been on the force. He told them how the Mounties were only three hundred strong when they began, three hundred men to patrol one of the biggest land masses on the planet, for a wage of seventy-five cents a day!

They sat spellbound when he told them about the time he'd found a snake in the boot he was about to put on; how he nearly drowned trying to save a kitten that had been washed away in a flood; how he was nearly trampled to death by a crazed bronco at a rodeo.

Now, the burden of these tales fell to Anna. The same little girls, the same soft light, the same attentive hush as Anna told and retold the tales they loved so much—but she wasn't Karl and never would be. Much as they loved their mother, the girls had been dazzled by their father.

Now, as she looked at them sitting side by side on the couch, their flannel nightgowns stretching all the way to the tiny pink feet that dangled off the edge of the couch, she thought how lucky she'd been when Karl was here— and she hadn't even known it. She'd always looked to the future, when they would have more money and thus more security, she'd never really just enjoyed the present.

Her empty bed told her that she'd been unappreciative. The lonely gray hours of dawn, when she used to rest her hand on sleeping Karl's hip, told her that she had unwisely overlooked all her blessings. And her two little girls, who could not quite ever get the sorrow from their eyes, told her she had been foolish not to appreciate what she'd had.

"Mom," the oldest girl said.

"Yes, hon?"

"Will you tell us about how the steamboat got stuck in the ice that time?"

"Isn't it getting late, hon?"

"I'm not tired at all." But then she spoiled the effect by taking her tiny hand and rubbing one of her eyes. Her little sister yawned.

"How about if I tell you that story tomorrow night?"

"I'm not tired, Mom, honest."

"Neither am I," said the youngest one. Then she yawned again.

Anna smiled. "You two are trying to fool me, aren't you?"

"No, Mom, honest. We're not tired at all."

"Just tell us a little bit," said the youngest one, "about the steamboat. Please?"

• • •

He looked through the french window.

Myra was right behind him. "What's goin' on in there?"

"The girls are sittin' on the couch. She's readin' to 'em."

"How cozy."

After the Mountie and the marshal had left, Myra had grabbed her coat, and they'd left the cathouse without even checking her office, which she usually did. Now they were standing outside the Swenson house, peering in.

In the light from the window, Myra Livermore and Gatineau looked like animals outcast from the paradise of soft lampglow and comfortable furnishings. Their features looked old and hard. In their eyes was just a hint of some of the things they'd done in their lives.

"She's a pretty one," Myra said, peeking around Gatineau and peering in at Anna.

Myra had always been curious about women like these—attractive if not beautiful with nice fashionably rounded bodies and a slight air of superiority that the wives of most important community men had about them. Myra thought how much she'd like to slap that air of superiority away. Then maybe Myra might have some things in common with the widow woman—

"You wanna go in now?" Gatineau said.

Myra smiled. "No. Let's give them a few more minutes. May as well give her a little peace. It'll be the last she has for a while."

Gatineau turned his head, staring at the woman. Most people tried to hide their dark side from you. Myra seemed happy to flaunt hers.

chapter
twenty-eight

LIZ CONWAY FOUND DAVID AND FRANK ADAMS at the Mountie cabin just getting ready to go out. When she came through the door, Kendricks, the Mountie who manned the post, smiled at the other two men. Mounties weren't used to pretty women walking through the door very often.

"I've been looking for you, Frank," Liz said.

"I'll take that as a compliment."

Liz laughed. "I'm glad you don't have much of an ego."

David said, "That's one thing my brother doesn't lack—self-confidence."

Kendricks went over to the stove and the coffee pot. He pointed to it. Liz nodded. After Liz had sipped her coffee—her skin was still red from the cold ride into town—she told Frank what she'd remembered about Karl Swenson's talk about the bridge.

"He didn't say which bridge?" Frank said.

"No, but there's only one that really matters around here," Liz said. Then, to Kendricks, "Right?"

"I'd say so. The bridge that connects the two parts of the Bay."

"He didn't say anything else about it?"

"He said 'The hell with them. They'll never find it.' "

"But he didn't say what 'it' was?"

"Not really."

"Would you care to guess what it might have been?"

Liz sipped her coffee, shrugged deep inside her sheep-lined jacket. "It was about the time of the bank robbery."

"But he didn't specifically say it was the bank robbery money?"

"No. Or if he did, I didn't hear him. He was pretty drunk, and he mumbled a lot."

"Probably worth checking out," David said.

"How about Anna Swenson? You still going over there?"

David nodded. "Right. And you can check out the bridge."

"Like to go with me?" Frank said.

"Sure," Liz Conway said.

"You're a lot prettier companion than my brother, anyway."

Kendricks said, "How about me? It's been damned dull around here lately." He pointed to a table covered with cards from a game of solitaire. "Playing cards by yourself can get pretty lonely."

David got up, straightened his red jacket, and put his hat on.

"I'll see you back here in an hour or so," he said.

He saluted Corporal Kendricks, who responded with a salute of his own, touched the brim of his hat as he passed Liz Conway, and went out into the chill evening.

Robinson couldn't help but laugh. Because it all seemed so crazy. This satchel he had in his hand as he walked along the moonlit road, looking out over the hoarfrost that silvered the open fields.

All his life he'd been one kind of slave or another and now, suddenly, he had power. Because that's what the money was. It wasn't good whiskey or blood-juicy steaks or perfumed whores. It was something more abstract—power.

It was, Yessir, Mr. Robinson, anything you say. Let me hold that door for you, Mr. Robinson. Sure is a fine night out tonight, isn't it now, Mr. Robinson.

He liked the sound of that. Just once he wanted to hear a white man call him that without mockery in his voice or eyes. Mr. Robinson.

Of course, they'd smirk behind his back and laugh about the foolish nigger. He expected that. But for just one moment to be treated like a complete human being—

And Jane was going to get the same kind of treatment. He was going to see to that.

He heard Myra's house before he saw it, the blare of laughter and player piano and girls giggling, like dervishes loosed out here on the prairie night. He walked faster, clutching the satchel even tighter.

In less than an hour from now, he expected to have Jane's hand in his and to be running through the darkness toward the rail depot four miles west of here. In the morning, a train would come and take both of them to a far better life than they'd ever known.

chapter
twenty-nine

WHILE MYRA LIVERMORE KNOCKED ON THE door, Gatineau stayed in the shadows of the front porch so that Anna Swenson would not see him when she answered the knock.

Anna looked puzzled when she opened the door, obviously not recognizing Myra. "Yes?"

"Good evening, Mrs. Swenson."

"Good evening to you."

"I wondered if I could come in and talk to you about something."

"Talk to me?" Now a certain anxiety joined Anna's puzzlement.

Behind Anna, Myra could see the nicely appointed living room, lampglow touching everything with a soft aura, the two little sisters sitting next to each other on the couch.

"My name is Myra Livermore."

Myra took pleasure in the shocked way people responded to her. Obviously Anna knew her by name. Anna looked as if somebody had given her a slight push. What would somebody like Myra Livermore be doing here?

"I won't need much of your time, ma'am."

"But I don't understand why you're here."

"Like I said, to talk."

"But about what?"

Myra smirked. "Your late husband."

Anna started to say something, then stopped herself. It was as if she'd had this sudden terrible thought that linked Karl and this terrible woman in front of her. My God, was there some kind of connection?

"Could you come back tomorrow?" Anna said. "I need to get the girls to bed now, and tomorrow would be much better."

That was when the grimy, powerful man stepped from the shadows of the porch and said, "We want to come inside now. We're tired of standin' out here."

Anna acted quickly, stepping back from the threshold, and starting to slam the door. But Gatineau was even quicker. He put his shoulder down and took a small run and slammed against the door so hard that, on the other side, Anna was knocked to the floor. The little girls screamed and ran to their mother. Soon they were clinging to her and crying.

Myra came through the door first, looking the place over calmly as if she might someday buy it. Gatineau was right behind her. He had his gun drawn. Closing the door behind him, Gatineau walked over to where the girls were hugging their mother and said, "You girls go back and sit where you were."

"You leave our mommy alone," the oldest girl said.

"You're a bad man," the other girl said.

Gatineau smiled with surprising warmth. He liked children, had always regretted in his shabby amoral way that he hadn't had any. "I'm not a bad man to nice little girls. Now, you go over on the couch and sit down and everything will be fine."

The girls looked at their mother, who was still sitting on the floor from her fall. Anna nodded to them and patted them on their backs reassuringly. The girls stared up at

Gatineau, then at Anna again. Then they walked over to the couch and sat down.

Anna got to her feet. She conveyed both fear and pure rage.

Myra said, "Where do you keep the whiskey in this place?"

"This is hardly a social call."

"I didn't say it was, bitch. I asked you where you kept the whiskey."

Myra slapped her with such force that Anna was driven back two feet. She seemed so stunned by the blow that she neither cried out nor said anything. She just looked shocked, as if the most terrible and unexpected thing in her life had just happened to her. The girls said nothing, either. They just watched, horrified.

Myra smiled at them. "You tell your mommy to be a nice mommy, and we'll get along fine." She turned back to Anna. "Now where's that whiskey?"

Saying nothing, Anna led the way from the living room, through the dining room with its long mahogany table shined to a fine luster, into the kitchen that smelled of nutmeg and ham and bread that had been baked earlier in the day.

Standing on her tiptoes, Anna reached up to the third shelf of a cupboard and retrieved a bottle of good sipping whiskey. The seal hadn't been broken. Obviously this was the kind of liquor kept for special occasions. Myra figured that her presence here marked this as a special occasion of some kind, anyway.

Without a word, Anna took down a clean glass, took it over to the counter, unsealed the bourbon, and poured a two-finger drink for Myra. She handed it to the woman.

Myra touched the long, graceful fingers bearing the drink.

"You have nice hands," Myra said, smiling.

For the second time in less than five minutes, the young widow seemed shocked by what she was seeing and hearing. First, a staggering slap to the face—something her own stern disciplinarian of a father had never visited on her— and now a sexual advance. Anna had heard of such women before but had never actually met one.

Anna found her voice. "Whatever you came here to say, I want you to say it here, in the kitchen, away from the girls."

"Isn't that sweet? Protecting her little daughters from the truth."

"I doubt you know anything about truth of any kind," Anna said.

Myra laughed. "You don't like me, do you?"

"No."

"You especially didn't like it when I touched your fingers."

"No, I didn't."

"You won't be such a high and mighty bitch when I tell you about your husband, believe me."

"I'm sure he had his faults," Anna said, sounding young and defensive despite herself.

And then they heard the laughter from the living room. Given the circumstances, the sound was startling.

Anna rushed through the shadows of the dining room to peek at the couch where the girls were. Gatineau was on his knees in front of the girls on the couch. He had one of their tiny orange balls balanced on the tip of his nose, and he was moving his head around, daring the little orange ball to fall off. He was as good at this trick as any circus performer Anna had ever seen.

The girls were young enough that they'd momentarily forgotten all that had transpired here over the past fifteen

COLD DEATH · 129

minutes. They were mesmerized by Gatineau and his trick. His gun was nowhere to be seen.

At first, Anna felt a curious sense of betrayal. Should the girls be so easily swayed by a man who was obviously an outlaw? But then she understood that they were responding as children needed to—rather than face the grim reality of the invaders, they'd elected to see at least one of the invaders as a nice, new friend.

As she watched Gatineau, she saw that he was actually enjoying himself.

"Stupid bastard," Myra said behind Anna. "I should have brought somebody else along."

Then she took Anna by the sleeve and turned her around, so that Anna was facing her. Myra put a rough hand on Anna's tender cheek. Anna wanted to throw up, but she knew better than to fight. Myra would just slap her again.

"You come back to the kitchen, honey. I got a lot of things to tell you about your husband."

Myra slid her hand down Anna's face so far that her elbow brushed against the young woman's breast. The elbow lingered there a moment.

"Sure don't know why he'd want to go cattin' around when he had somethin' as nice 'n juicy as you at home," Myra said. She shoved Anna back in the general direction of the kitchen.

chapter
thirty

THEY STARTED WITH THE BRIDGE ITSELF, PACING off half each, searching for any place that something might have been hidden. But construction was tight. They found no hiding places.

They met in the middle of the bridge. It was dark, and the cold, hard wind chafed the skin.

"Maybe it wasn't this bridge," Liz Conway said.

"Or maybe he didn't mean on top of the bridge."

"Below?"

"Worth a try."

He stood a moment looking across the shiny black river dotted with the watercolor tints of the town's lights. From here, the town of Kelly Bay looked big and prosperous, and he had a sudden, vagrant need to belong to something, something that a U.S. Marshal traveling constantly never experienced.

"You all right?"

He tilted his head to her and nodded.

"You're an interesting man, you know that?"

And then she was in his arms, and they were both doing what they'd wanted to do the whole time he was out at her cabin. She felt warm and right, and her mouth tasted familiar, a taste of an old girlfriend suddenly remembered. He kept kissing her until he could feel the goosebumps on her neck.

"Maybe we'd better get to work," he said.

"Maybe I'd rather do this." She smiled. "I like it."

"So do I. But I still think we'd better get to work."

She laughed and touched her head to his chest. "I knew you were going to say that." Then she shook her head. "Lord save me from dedicated men."

They walked to the closest end of the bridge and started the descent down the hoarfrosted slope leading to the water.

The girl wondered when the first one would be here tonight. Just before they started, the girl always took a few quick harsh drinks of whiskey. Made what she was about to do a little less shameful, a little less painful. They didn't care that she was young and couldn't really accommodate them. They just went ahead and did it anyway.

The girl lay on the bed, sipping the whiskey that Myra always gave her in pints—one pint for each week—thinking about Robinson and his promise. Where was he? Had something happened to him? Had Myra somehow caught on to what Robinson was doing and stopped him?

The wind rattled the windows in the dark attic, and the naked branches clawed like begging children on the glass. Where was Robinson, anyway?

The girl lay her head down and fell into fitful sleep.

Robinson had to be careful. Now that he had the satchel of money, all he needed was the key to the girl's chain, then they could be on their way.

All he could think of was America, a city up north where he and the girl could find a place to live, even though, truth be told, white folks were no kinder to his type in the North than they were in the South. Still and all, he could get them a nice apartment that was sunny in the mornings and breezy at night, and he could see that she grew up righteous, the way a young girl of any color should grow up.

He crept down the shadowy hall, looking both ways. While the house was up and running for the night, and while Myra's office was in the center of a seldom-used hall, there was always the possibility that he would be spotted by one of the whores. To keep on Myra's good side, they were constantly reporting things that Robinson did or didn't do. They didn't like him because his contempt for them was so obvious. One night, one of them had even told Myra that Robinson had raped her, but she forgot about Myra's way of learning the truth quickly. Not wanting to lose Robinson if she didn't have to—he was a good employee—Myra grabbed the girl by her tits.

Myra's method was to twist their tits until they started crying. If they stuck to their story through all that pain, Myra figured they were telling the truth. But if they were lying, well, they pretty much always fessed up once Myra started twisting.

He reached Myra's door. He slid his black hand on the burnished brass doorknob. He took the key he'd stolen earlier in the day by waiting until Myra had been called upstairs then slipping in through the door before she got back. He opened the office door.

He went inside, closing the door softly behind him. He set the satchel down on the floor. No way would he let that satchel ever get more than three feet away from him.

The blinds made bars of the moonlight. He could smell her whiskey and her cigars and her perfume, that odd mixture of female and male he disliked about her.

He went straight to her roll-top desk and a small drawer that he'd seen her open one day just as she was leaving to go up for the attic. Robinson was a man who noticed things, small things, and many times this came in handy. He opened the small drawer, and there, lying in the center of it, was a lone key, a heavy brass key. He put it in his hand and closed the drawer. He was about to step lightly to the door when he heard something.

Given the immediate noise of player piano and laughter, and the distant noise of wind, he wasn't sure what the sound had been. Or even if it was a sound worth getting excited about. But something close by—

He waited. Sweat dripped from his brow. His stomach felt sick, his bowels cramped. His ears tried to penetrate the various sounds, making distinctions between them, trying to discern anything untoward or ominous.

Nothing. He was safe. He was sure of it. He picked up the satchel. He stepped across to the door and opened it up, and that was when a very tiny whore put a very big .45 right into his face.

"Now you just get right back in there, nigger," she said, "or I'll blow your black brains out."

chapter
thirty-one

ROBINSON PUT HIS HANDS UP OBEDIENTLY—IT
had been a long life of servitude and obedience and sometimes he grew so weary of it that he simply wanted to sit
down and die—and he was just backing up into the office
when Jody snapped, "What was that?"

"What was what?"

"That noise."

"Didn't hear no noise, ma'am," Robinson said.

But Jody was obviously remembering earlier in the evening when she'd heard somebody rummaging around in here.
But then Jody had been called away and hadn't been able
to find out if it was really somebody or—

"Stand aside. I had one of the girls standin' watch in the
hall. She said she thought she heard somethin' in here."

"Huh?"

"You heard me, nigger. Stand aside."

Robinson sighed, having no idea what was going on here,
just afraid that his entire plan was going to come undone.
He should have known better than to have any hope for
himself or the child in the attic. For people like them, hope
was the spiritual equivalent of fool's gold.

"Come out of there," Jody said.

Robinson looked at her as if she were insane. Who the
hell was she talking to anyway?

Jody moved with no warning, plunging three steps to the closet door and then flinging it backwards. Like a harlequin in a jack-in-the-box, Rosarita came jumping out of the shadows in the closet. She went straight for Jody, big homely hands going right for the whore's throat.

Robinson had never seen Rosarita look this way—crazed, being the only word for it. The two women struggled like bear wrestlers. Rosarita was smart and tied up Jody's gun hand so the whore couldn't squeeze a shot off. Jody pushed Rosarita back against the desk. The whore was just raising the gun to fire when Rosarita's left foot came up from nowhere and just about kicked the gun from Jody's hand.

Then Jody surprised both Robinson and Rosarita by gripping the barrel of the gun in her hand and using the handle as a club. She threw herself at Rosarita and began slamming the pearl handle of the six-shooter hard against Rosarita's temple. Three, four, five times the Mexican woman was hit.

The last time there was a tiny whimper from Rosarita, and then, in the darkness, Robinson could see the whites of her eyes turn to an eerie gray, and Rosarita collapsed to the floor.

Jody, infuriated and drugged with her own violence, fell to her knees and continued hammering Rosarita's skull. Robinson would have tried to stop her, but he knew he was already too late. Rosarita had died a few minutes ago.

Jody, hearing Robinson start to move again, whirled around and pointed the business end of the gun directly at his heart. The handle was sticky with blood and brain matter but Jody didn't seem to notice. All she said was, the six-shooter still aimed directly at Robinson's heart, "One move nigger, and you're dead. You understand me?"

chapter
thirty-two

JUST AS HE WALKED INTO THE AREA LIGHTED by the porch lantern, David Adams's mounted police jacket became red. He walked straight up to the door and knocked. A mother with two young girls was probably up at this hour. Given all the work required to keep two growing girls properly raised, she'd almost have to be up cooking or darning or laying out the next day's clothes.

He knocked three times. There was no answer. He put his ear to the door, listened. He heard nothing but the chill, soughing wind.

He wasn't sure why, but something suddenly seemed wrong.

He was a bad man, then he was a nice man. Now he was a bad man again.

The girls sat watching as the man named Gatineau quit balancing the ball on his nose and jumped to his feet right after the first knock. He went to the wall on the other side of the door, flattened himself against it, and then once again drew his huge, vicious-looking gun.

The girls were scared. They knew for sure now that he was a bad man. He'd only been pretending to be a nice man. Just pretending.

A minute later, the girls saw Myra shove their mother

into the room. Their mother reached down, took their hands, and held them close to her face. Myra gave her another shove, this time toward the door.

Their mother composed herself, patted her hair, tugged down on her dress, and took a very deep breath. She looked anxiously at Myra, who had pressed herself against the wall right next to Gatineau.

There was another knock, the fourth. Myra nodded to their mother.

Anna Swenson reached down, took the doorknob in her hand, glanced again at Myra, and then opened the door.

David Adams wasn't sure, but he had the impression something was wrong the moment the door opened and Anna stood there, soft and pretty in the lampglow.

"Hello, David."

"Hello. I wondered if I could come in."

Her hesitation—and the way her eyes flicked to the left—made him wonder again if everything was all right.

"Of course. I'd love to see you." With that, she stood back and held the door for him.

Gatineau took a deep breath. Hitting a Mountie was going to be fun, even if he had sworn he'd always stay out of trouble with the redcoats. He raised his big hand and his even bigger weapon so that it would fall like a guillotine on the back of the Mountie's neck.

David knew that he was going to have to move quickly, so just as the toe of his boot touched the threshold, he drew his weapon, pushed Anna out of the way to safety, turned, and fired at the owner of the huge shadow that had moments before appeared on the rug before David. David got off two shots, one to the head, one to the chest.

Gatineau's arms went wide, almost in a parody of the crucifixion, and he was hurled back hard against the wall.

He was a shambles of a man, dirty, greasy, mean-looking, and he died in just about the way you'd expect, crying out for a mercy he'd seldom shown others, terrified of the great black void he'd sent many other into ahead of him.

"David!" Anna screamed.

But before David could turn and address himself to Anna's cry for help, Myra had time to grab the oldest girl and put a gun to her head.

"Now, Mountie," Myra said, "you put that gun down, or I'm going to shoot this little bitch right on the spot."

chapter
thirty-three

THIRTY-FIVE MINUTES AFTER THEY STARTED
searching the bridge, Frank Adams carried his lantern up
the steep slope beneath the west end of it and found the spot
that had recently been dug up. He shouted for Liz Conway,
then started digging.

His knees were soon wet from the muddy earth, and the
smell of dog shit up here was nearly overpowering. The
only interesting thing the lantern light revealed was a series
of dirty words that some boys had chalked on the span of
steel along the bottom of the bridge itself.

He kept digging.

"Good Lord," Liz Conway said, breathless from running
over here, curious about the hole he was digging.

"Somebody dug all this up very recently," he explained.
"Maybe even earlier tonight. You can see how fresh the
dirt is."

"You want me to help?"

Frank was always grateful for a helping hand. "I'd appreciate it."

She got down on the other side of the hole and started
digging, too.

"Do you think this is where the money could be?"

"Possibly," Frank said.

They kept digging.

"Isn't this a pretty public place to hide something?"

"Not really. Unless folks around Kelly Bay act very different from other people, nobody much walks under a bridge like this except for maybe some kids and a few fishermen."

He pointed to the hole. "I'm sure this was covered up with something. When I found it tonight, it was just some freshly dug dirt. But say something had been on top of it— who'd knock it over to look underneath? Probably nobody." He looked around at the barren slope with its tufts of brown grass, its dog turds, and its dirty words. "This is probably a pretty good place to hide something, actually."

She nodded, and they got back to work.

Frank was trying to figure out how Karl Swenson had gotten involved in hiding the money stolen from his own bank. No matter what answer Frank came up with, Karl looked pretty bad. Somehow, he'd at least had knowledge of the robbery and, for some reason, had chosen to hide the money up here.

When they got to the bottom of the hole, they found it empty. Liz knelt on her knees, brushing sweat beads from her forehead with one finger of her glove. She also kept trying to push back an errant piece of hair that kept falling in her face.

"Any ideas?"

"Just the obvious one," Frank said.

"I guess I'm dumb. What's the obvious one?"

"Somebody beat us here. And probably not very long ago."

"So right now somebody has the bank robbery money?"

"Most likely," Frank said.

Frank walked downslope so he could stand up without banging his head against the underside of the bridge.

He looked out at the sleek surface of the river, black and cold in the moonlight.

Liz came up from behind him and slid her arms around his waist. "What're you thinking about?"

"How none of this makes sense."

She laughed softly. "That's just what I was thinking."

"And one more thing."

"What's that?"

"That if Karl Swenson was involved in the robbery, why did he have to hide the money from his accomplices?"

"You think that's who was up there digging tonight? His accomplices?"

"I guess I don't know who else it could have been."

Liz walked around from behind him. This time when she slid her arms around his waist, she put his face right up next to his. "I'm really a very shy lady."

"I believe it."

"Do you really?"

"Actually, I do."

"Then how do you explain how forward I'm being tonight?"

He smiled. "I guess I can't explain it. But I'll tell you one thing."

"What's that?"

"You don't hear me complaining any, do you?"

A few minutes later, both wishing this were another time, another place, they started walking back to the Mountie post.

"You two look cold," Corporal Kendricks said when they reached the Mountie cabin.

Liz went immediately for the coffee pot on the cast iron stove.

Frank said, "My brother back yet?"

Kendricks looked up from the yellowback he'd been reading. There was a pen-and-ink drawing on the cover depicting a white man in fancy cowboy attire holding a six-shooter on a red man in fancy Indian attire.

"Haven't seen him yet," Kendricks said.

"He's probably just talking to Anna," Liz Conway said. "I'm sure it isn't easy, asking her about Karl that way."

Frank nodded. That sounded like a reasonable explanation. No reason to worry about his kid brother, though he frequently did. Just as Liz said, David was probably just talking to Anna Swenson.

Frank gratefully accepted the steaming cup of coffee Liz handed him.

chapter
thirty-four

JODY'S STORY WAS PRETTY TYPICAL OF THE girls found in bawdy houses. A runaway from a Kentucky farm at sixteen, she drifted north with the rail lines, finally ending up, at nineteen, in Montreal where Myra had "discovered" her working the streets. Myra had told her of a "better" life, which Jody at first had mistaken for the fantasy of a horny old madame, but Myra was persuasive, and Jody had returned with her to Kelly Bay—and damned if Myra hadn't been telling the truth, life in Myra's was in fact a better life.

Jody soon developed a specialty, an oral one, after Myra pointed out that girls who learned to be especially proficient at certain things were bound to make more money. So Jody became extraordinarily skilled at certain man-pleasing skills, and she did indeed make more money. In fact, some of the other girls were jealous of her and called her Myra's pet. Jody didn't care. From Myra, she had learned ambition, and these days she put all her ambition to work.

She was Myra's number one snitch, for one thing. If anything untoward went on in the house, Jody told Myra. If anybody complained unduly about the set-up here, Jody told Myra. Any girl who even hinted that she occasionally went into town and did a little business on the sly, Jody told Myra.

Myra trusted Jody completely, and even though Myra
had long ago tired of Jody sexually—Myra had an insatiable
craving for "fresh new meat to carve," as a poet had once
said—they were still good friends and confidantes. Whenever Myra was gone, Jody watched over the place with a
ruthless eye, which is how she had come to catch Robinson
creeping down the hallway toward Myra's office and had
watched him with glee as he snuck inside and closed the
door behind him, thinking he was all safe and sound and
getting away with his thievery.

Now, she held her gun directly in Robinson's face.
"What're you looking for?"

Robinson hung his head. "Just a little money. Thought
I'd go into town and put a little drunk on."

She stepped over Rosarita's corpse and slapped him.
Even a black man should be able to invent a better lie
than that one. Especially Robinson, who was damn smart
when you came right down to it.

"Now tell me the truth."

Myra's office was still dark, moonlight in bars through
the blinds falling across the floor.

The music of the player piano and the laughter floated
down the hall.

"I was lookin' for money, like I told you."

"Bullshit. You better tell me the truth, Robinson, because
otherwise Myra's gonna kick your ass when she gets back
here."

Robinson smiled. "She gonna kick my ass anyway."

And then Jody saw the satchel on the floor leaning next
to Robinson's leg. For one thing, the top of the satchel had
been reinforced with leather. A fancy lock held the two
sides of the satchel together beneath the leather handles.
"What's in the satchel?"

"Huh?"

"Don't go dumb on me. You know what I'm talkin' about."

"Just some things."

She could see how tense Robinson suddenly was.

"What kind of things?"

"Just old clothes, things like that. Just takin' 'em down to my room."

"With the bank's name on it? Give it to me," Jody said.

"It's mine, Miss Jody. I got a right to my things."

"You give it to me, Robinson, or I'll shoot you right here. All I'll have to say is you got fresh with me, and I had to kill you to keep your dirty black hands off my pure white body." Jody laughed at her own humor. She waved the gun at him again. "Now pick up that satchel, Robinson, and hand it over here, you understand me?"

She could see him gulp. She could see him look down at the satchel longingly, as if it were the most precious thing in all the world, and then look back up at her.

"You open to a deal, Miss Jody?"

"What kind of deal?"

"A deal that could give you a lot of money just for lettin' me walk out of here."

"How much money?"

"A lot of money, Miss Jody. More money than you ever seen before, I promise you that."

She knew better than to even start seriously considering his offer. For one thing, no black man could ever have come across that much money. For another thing, anybody who ever betrayed Myra would pay for it with her life. No matter how long it took, Myra would hunt you down and kill you.

"You just hand me that satchel, Robinson, and you do it right now."

Robinson shook his old black head and made a clucking sound and reached down with a great air of resignation to lift the satchel up and give it to Miss Jody.

He brought up the satchel all right, brought it up so hard and so fast that before she could even squeeze off a shot, he'd clubbed her directly on the side of the head with the satchel. She heard herself scream—but who else was going to hear her with all the noise going on? Then a great cold swimming darkness overtook her senses.

She felt herself crumpling to the floor.

chapter
thirty-five

TWO YEARS AGO, ONE WARM SPRING NIGHT, Myra Livermore was surprised to see a new face among the men at her whorehouse. There were new men all the time, of course—Myra's bawdyhouse was almost mandatory among the important men in this wedge of the province—but seldom were the men, like this man, president of the local bank. A man like that took a great chance just by crossing her threshold, and she immediately considered him reckless and therefore lesser for showing up here. He had too much to lose to gamble it all on a piece of tail.

Nonetheless, Myra feigned great delight in seeing him here and invited him to sample two or three of her best girls. Three nights later, he was back again, even drunker this time than he'd been the last. She now saw him as something of a pretender, an insecure drunk, and not a real leader at all. The real leaders would never come here, only that group of men just below the real leaders. But one thing was for sure—she knew she would someday, in some way, find Mr. Swenson to be useful.

It was not until his third month of visits that he brought up the attic. Like many of her frequent customers, Karl Swenson had seen her go up to the attic, and he was naturally curious about what was up there, especially after he twice saw a man accompany her, a man he knew to be a customer. That was when he started pestering her about the attic. She didn't tell most men about the upstairs room because she was afraid the word would get around town and the Mounties would come out, look for themselves, and put her in jail for abusing the rights of a minor. The Mounties tended to let whorehouses slide if no children were involved, but if Jane were discovered, Myra would be fated for jail. She let Swenson stay longer than the usual twenty minutes in the attic. She figured it would all come in handy some day.

He went up there the first time on a snowy Tuesday night. He didn't come down for six hours. He was back the next night and the next and the next. He had no shame or sense of the trouble he was getting himself in. He was so naïve, he didn't seem to understand the power he was yielding to Myra. While the girl was much older than she looked, she was still trouble for a bank president.

Shortly after this, he began bringing Jane flowers, and candy, and small jeweled trinkets. Myra had decided that not only was he a lightweight as far as business, he was weak inside. It was one thing to want sex with a tight-skinned young girl—Myra enjoyed that same sort of sex herself—but it was something else to be bedeviled by a little whore.

The curious thing was, Jane began to ask for Karl, too. She told Myra that he was the only man who had ever treated her decently. When she showed Myra some of the presents he'd brought her, Jane was so moved, she cried.

About a year and a half into this peculiar relationship, Myra got the idea for the bank robbery. She had long held the dream of someday just vanishing, of living the rest of her life in Europe, where she would pamper herself with the fine things she figured she deserved after all these years of toil. What better grubstake than a bankful of money?

She managed to get Karl sober one night—two and a half pots of coffee, with him pissing every five minutes— and then she told him her plans. She just sat in her office chair and leaned forward, palms flat on her knees, and told him exactly what he was going to do. Didn't ask. Didn't bribe. Didn't wheedle. Just told him straight out what he was going to do. Or else she was going to tell everybody, including the bank's Board of Directors and his very own wife, exactly what he'd been up to and with whom.

She said, "Next Thursday, late in the day, Robinson is going to come into your bank with a mask on and a gun in his hand. He's going to come directly to your office and demand that you open the vault and give him the money. Then he's going to slip out the side door, and you're going to fire at him twice and miss both times. He's going to get away, and we're going to split the money, you and me. Do you understand me, Mr. Bank President?"

What choice did he have? He went along.

Came next Thursday, he sat in his office waiting for Robinson, who wore a party mask that covered his entire face, collar up and gloves on so that nobody could see that his skin was black. Robinson showed up on time. He came straight through the side door and went into Swenson's office.

Everybody in the bank saw the pantomimed performance. Robinson, waved the gun around, Swenson put his hands up in the air, Robinson pointed with his gun to the vault, and Swenson obliged him by piling all the money into a hefty satchel. Toting the satchel, Robinson ran out the side door. Swenson followed. As planned, he fired twice, the sound booming inside the small bank, the drifting gray gunsmoke gritty and acrid on the air.

The only thing Myra didn't know about was Swenson's own plan. He went out the side door, jumped on a horse, and rode after Robinson. This time, he shot at Robinson for real. Robinson knew enough to halt his horse. He knew that Swenson, who looked crazed, would kill him. Swenson took the satchel. Robinson rode out to Myra's and told her what had happened.

It came down to this: Swenson had cleverly double-crossed them. He had taken the money and hidden it for himself. If Myra went to the law, she'd have to implicate herself in the robbery as well as Swenson. So, drunk though he was, degenerate though he was, Swenson had proved to be a lot smarter than Myra had thought.

Then Swenson had been left to face his demons. The man who at one time had been a Mountie was now a thief, a drunkard, and a whoremaster. He had betrayed his family, he had betrayed his own ideals. He would have turned the money in, but then everybody would have known about his part in the robbery, and the shame would be too much for Anna. So he left the money where he had hidden it.

And one night, so ashamed that he could no longer tolerate living, he slipped from bed and went outside to the shed, doused himself in kerosene, and set himself on fire.

Myra related all this with relish. The pain her story caused Anna was easy to see. She hated women like Anna.

Myra stood in the middle of the living room, still holding the oldest daughter hostage.

"So what do you think of your husband now?"

"I just want you to let my daughter go," Anna said, obviously trying to hold her tears. Myra had had enough satisfaction already.

"I'll let her go as soon as you tell me where the money is," Myra said.

"I don't know where it is. How many times do I have to tell you that?"

Myra pushed the gun against the girl's head. "You know how fast I could kill her?"

The girl started crying.

"Please," Anna said. "Please don't hurt her."

"Then tell me. And you better make it fast."

Anna raised her eyes to David's. "Should I tell her, David?"

He immediately knew what she was trying to do. "I guess you don't have any choice."

Anna looked back at Myra. "All right. I'll tell."

Myra smirked. "I knew you weren't tough enough to hold out, honey. I knew it. Now show me where that money is."

Anna sighed and said, "It's upstairs. In the closet in the den."

David knew what Anna was doing, of course. He just hoped there'd be some chance to overpower Myra once they got upstairs—overpower her without getting the girl killed.

chapter
thirty-six

FRANK ADAMS SAID, "HE'S BEEN GONE AN AWFUL long time."

Kendricks looked up from his yellowback. He was just at the part where the sheriff was personally killing somewhere in the vicinity of sixty or seventy crazed Indian warriors. The sheriff was one hell of a shot, not to mention a man with nerves of steel. "I guess you're right. It is kind of funny that he's been gone this long, now that you mention it."

"Why don't we go over there? It's not far," Liz Conway said.

Frank winked at Kendricks. "Did you catch the 'we'? Meet my new assistant."

Kendricks, good clean-cut farmboy that he was, came immediately to Liz's defense. "Sure wish I had an assistant that pretty."

Frank smiled at Liz. "Now that you mention it, I guess I am pretty damn lucky after all."

Frank went over and got his coat, took down Liz's and helped her into it. "We should be back here in a little while, Kendricks."

Kendricks held up his yellowback. "Well, I've got things to keep myself occupied with."

Frank grinned. "You're a credit to the Mounties."

Once outside, Liz said, "Are you really worried about David?"

"He's been gone a while. It may be that they're just talking. On the other hand—" He shrugged. His right hand dropped instinctively to the .44 riding his hip. "On the other hand, it could always be something else, I guess."

Liz noticed that Frank's strides got longer and his face tenser in the moonlight. She could see his jaw working. He seemed worried. They hurried on their way to Anna Swenson's house, their bootheels loud on the boardwalk.

Robinson opened Myra's office door and peeked out. Down at the end of the hall, a portly man was eagerly feeling up a buxom whore. He had his hand plunged down the front of her spangled dress, and he appeared to be licking her lips every few seconds. Robinson wondered how the girl could stand it. The man looked to be a pure drunken pig.

Robinson glanced back to Jody on the floor. She was snoring now, a raw and ragged sound in the darkness of Myra's office. He'd hit her hard with the satchel, and the blow had done its job.

He just wished the sonofabitch down at the end of the hall would take the girl upstairs and get it over with. Robinson wanted to get to the attic, get Jane, and get them both out of here.

He waited. Patience had never been one of his virtues.

Myra said, "All right, where is it?"

"At the end of the hall."

It had taken them five minutes to get up the stairs. Anna had gone first, then David, then Myra holding the oldest daughter. The younger daughter was tied up and in the kitchen. Myra had been afraid that the girl would sneak out and run for help.

By now, Myra seemed pretty much convinced that she was going to find the money just where Anna had said, in the closet in the den. Now, careful to keep the gun tight to the girl's head, Myra said, "You go get it for me."

Anna looked shocked, her eyes flicking to David's in pure panic. Her plan had been so simple. Woo Myra upstairs and when the opportunity presented itself, jump her, and free the girl. But Anna had underestimated Myra's cunning.

David said, "I'll go get the money and bring it back to you."

Myra's eyes narrowed. "Why you and not Anna?"

"She wants to stay with her daughter. Can't you see how scared she is?"

Obviously, Myra didn't like it, but she didn't put up any real objection.

The hall was narrow. The only light was from the small, flickering lantern that Anna carried.

David said, "I'm going to go down there and get the money, and I'm going to bring it back to you and I don't want you to hurt either one of them. Do you understand?"

Myra smirked. "Aren't we noble in our nice red uniform?"

"Do you understand me, Myra?" David repeated, careful to hold his temper.

"You just go get the money, Mr. Mountie, and bring it back here. I'll worry about everything else."

David reached out and took Anna's hand, holding it for a long moment. Her eyes said, What are you going to do, David? How are we going to get out of this situation? All David could do was offer her a fleeting smile that he hoped she found reassuring.

He turned back to Myra and the girl, put his hand on the girl's head, and smiled at her. She looked frail and vulnerable and terrified in the lantern light. "Everything will be all right, honey," he said.

But as he turned around and started walking down the hall, he thought, All right, Mr. Hero, now what the hell are you going to do? How're you going to get that kid away from Myra without getting the kid killed? It was a good question. He just wished he had a good answer.

He walked straight down the hallway to the den.

An old French priest, Father Marquette, who had run a city soup kitchen, had taught Jane how to pray. As she waited for Robinson to come and get her, she prayed that Robinson was all right and that he would be here soon.

Her ankle was bloody. Some nights she felt a real panic, being restrained this way, so she started working her ankle against the metal that bound her to the chain. The metal was always stronger than she was, and her ankle would be gnawed raw.

Hail Mary full of grace. Our Father Who art in heaven. Glory be to the Father and the Son and to the Holy Ghost.

Her prayers were soft in the chill darkness of the attic, moonlight silver across her rumpled bedclothes, and across her slender girlish body.

Please help Robinson, Lord. Please help Robinson.

She waited. There was nothing else to do.

chapter
thirty-seven

THE DEN WAS SO DARK THAT DAVID BUMPED against an armchair when he stepped across the threshold. In the moonlight, the room looked pleasant and homey, with bookshelves and a desk and a comfortable reading chair. He wished that his old friend Karl Swenson had spent more time here and less time chasing his adolescent inclinations.

He looked back down the hall. Myra and the girl appeared almost ghostly in the jittery lantern light. Only the silver gun appeared formidable and real. David tried not to think about what the girl's head would look like if Myra pulled the trigger. He had no doubt that Myra was perfectly capable of doing it.

He crossed the room, found the closet, and opened the door. The tall, angular room smelled of moth balls.

David got down on his hands and knees and began searching for anything that would look as if it could hold a great deal of money. He found a stack of books for which there was apparently no room on the shelves, a pair of winter lace-up boots, and a box containing framed photographs, the glass sleek and cold to the touch. In other words, he found nothing useful.

He stood up, knees cracking in the gloom, and started searching around the room.

"What the hell're you doin' down there?" Myra shouted.

"Won't be long," David shouted back. But it would be long if he couldn't find something to deceive her with. He needed to find it damned fast.

The portly fart finally lifted his hand from the girl's dress, licked her face a few more times, then took her hand and led her upstairs. Lucky girl.

Robinson moved. He had the key, and he had the cash. Soon he would have the girl, and they would both have their freedom.

Closing the door behind him, leaving Jody still snoring on the floor, Robinson moved quickly down the shadowy hallway to the staircase. He carried the satchel right along with him. No way it was going to leave his sight or his grasp. No way at all.

The girls and their johns were too busy to notice him. In a curious way, blacks were invisible to white people. For once, Robinson was grateful for this curious phenomenon.

He went up the stairs, past all the drunken revelers pawing and being pawed, getting drunk, pretending to a hilarity that probably hid great sorrow they did not choose to recognize in themselves.

On the second floor landing, one of the whores stopped him and said that a man had puked in her room and she wanted Robinson to go clean it up. He said it would be a little while.

She didn't look happy about this. "I'm going to tell Myra," she said and flounced off.

Fuck Myra, Robinson thought, and it gave him a good feeling. Fuck Myra.

A few minutes later, he was on the third floor and headed down the hallway to the door leading to the attic. This was where he had to be careful. He didn't want anybody see him going up there.

He had to wait—people were coming and going in the rooms—until the hallway was empty. When the hallway was clear, he put the key in the lock, opened the door, jumped into the darkness, and then closed the door. He stood in the gloom, out of breath, sweating, oddly chilled. Then he turned around and started up the slanting, dusty steps to the attic.

He was about to free a slave. It felt good, real good.

chapter
thirty-eight

AS THEY DREW NEAR THE SWENSON HOUSE, Frank Adams pointed to the second floor and said, "Look."

Liz Conway squinted in the darkness and said, "What?"

"Anna Swenson is just standing in the hallway."

"What's wrong with that?"

"It just seems funny."

"Because she's just standing there?"

"Right. She should be doing something."

"Like what?"

"Putting the girls to bed or taking down her hair for the night—something."

"What're you going to do?"

"Let's sneak up on the house and peek in the ground-floor windows."

"I'm glad you're a lawman, otherwise we could get arrested for this."

He smiled. "Very funny."

They set off for the house, pushing past the slapping, thick branches of fir trees. There was a light in the living room, so they went to these windows first. Everything looked orderly and neat, but there was no sign of anybody.

Frank wondered where David was. He was getting a feeling in his stomach he didn't like. They'd been looking through the west windows. Ducking down, they hunched their way over to the east windows. Frank rose up slowly, carefully, in case somebody inside was watching. He looked in the window.

There was a dead man sprawled on the living room floor. A great deal of blood had soaked into the rug. Beneath his breath, Frank cursed.

"What's wrong?" Liz Conway whispered.

"Take a look."

She eased herself up to peer in the window.

"My God," she said, when she was crouching next to Frank again.

"They're on the second floor. I've got to get up there."

"But how? They'll hear you coming up the stairs."

"Yeah, but with the wind they may not hear me climbing up the lattice on the side."

"Can you make it?"

"My brother's up there. I've got to make it."

Jane looked up when she heard Robinson at the top of the stairs. She had been lost in her prayers.

"Guess what I got?" Robinson said. He couldn't stop himself from grinning.

"You really got it, Robinson? You really got the key?"

And like a magician, Robinson made the key appear magically in his dark fingers. It seemed to glow in the pale moonlight.

Without another word, he crossed the room, the aged boards creaking, knelt down next to her, found the lock on the metal cuff, and freed her.

"Oh, Robinson!" she said, and threw her arms around him, the way she would have her own father.

"Now you put on your warmest clothes, and we'll get going," Robinson said.

She had been chained so long that she limped some as she moved around the room, finding her warmest clothes. These turned out to be a sweater and a cotton dress. Myra had always kept the girl half-naked because that was the way both Myra and her customers liked Jane to be.

And then they were ready.

"You gonna miss this old place?" Robinson said.

"Sure," Jane said. "I'm gonna miss it a lot."

Robinson laughed. "It's gonna be better for both of us down in America. I promise you that."

"Thanks for helping me, Robinson. I can't tell you how much I appreciate it."

"I want you to grow up the right way. That's how you can show me how much you appreciate it."

Then Robinson leaned over to an upended trunk and picked up a big floppy picture hat.

"Put this on," he said.

"How come?"

"I don't want nobody here to see your face. We got to move fast before they figure out what's going on."

She put the hat on. Robinson pulled it down so that the slant of the soft straw brim covered most of her face.

"There," he said. "Even I wouldn't recognize you."

Robinson picked up the money satchel, and they set off.

This was going to be the trickiest part of all, getting past all the girls without them knowing what was going on. At least Myra wasn't here, he thought.

They went down the stairs. Robinson put his head to the door and listened. This was taking a big chance, but he had no choice, he had to assume that because he heard no noise close by, this end of the hallway was empty.

"You ready?" he whispered.

"I'm scared."

"Won't be long now. We'll be safe. You'll see."

"I love you, Robinson. You're like my father."

Robinson eased the door open. He saw her right away, Jody, the whore he'd knocked out downstairs. She had a big Remington breech-load double-barrel shotgun. She stood right in front of him.

She didn't say anything. She didn't hesitate. She gave him both barrels point blank in the face. Jane started screaming.

Jody stepped back so Robinson would have room to fall. He was dead before his body touched the floor.

chapter
thirty-nine

THE LATTICE THREATENED TO CRUMBLE BE-
neath his weight, but Frank Adams kept climbing. His only
hope was to reach the second floor of the Swenson house,
find a window, and sneak in. The wind bit his face. His
muscles cramped from moving so slowly and carefully. He
tried to make no noise whatsoever.

He just hoped he could get inside in time. He kept
thinking about the dead man on the living-room floor. He
hoped his brother David was all right.

"You come out of there and right now."

"All right."

All David had been able to find was a long, narrow canvas
bag that Karl Swenson had kept from his Mountie days. Karl
had always kept most of his belongings in there. David had
stuffed it full of newspapers and magazines, hoping that
they would convince Myra, at least momentarily, that he
had found the money.

But then what? How was he ever going to get any of them
free? He had no doubt that Myra planned to kill them all.

He started down the hall. Anna's head snapped around.
Her eyes watched David carefully. She looked as if she
really wanted believe that he had come up with some way
to get them out of this—but knew that he hadn't. Because

there was no way. Myra had the gun and the girl.

"You get it?" Myra said.

"Right here," David said, hoisting the canvas bag.

"Bring it here," Myra said.

Now what? David thought. Now what?

Frank's foot went through one of the lattice squares. He stopped, afraid that he might have been heard. He resumed climbing again.

When he came to a window to the right of the lattice, he peered inside. Darkness. Only a faint flicker of lantern light from the hallway. It was going to be a reach—the window was at least two and a half feet from the lattice.

He stretched, feeling his groin tighten, and found a handle. Getting enough leverage to push up the window wasn't easy but he finally managed it. Now began the long process of feeding himself across the two and a half feet separating him from the square opening of window. He started crawling across the side of the house.

"Put it down right there, open it up, and show me the money."

David and Anna glanced at each other. He could see in her eyes that she knew this was nothing more than a trick, that they would soon all be dead, including her daughters.

"You hear what I said? Open it up," Myra said.

What choice did David have? He knelt down and started to open it up.

Once he was inside, his crotch afire from the strain of climbing through the window, Frank took out his .44 and crept on tiptoes to the door. He saw the situation: he was behind a woman who held a kid and a gun to the kid's head.

Anna and David were down the hall. David had knelt down and was about to open a long, narrow canvas bag.

Frank said, "You put that gun down, lady, or I'm going to blow your head off your shoulders."

David and Anna peered into the darkness behind Myra.

David recognized his brother's voice immediately.

"He'll kill you, Myra. He really will," David said.

"I'll get the girl first," Myra said.

"No, you won't," Frank said. "And you know you won't."

Myra moved quickly for an older lady of her size. She started to turn around, so that she could use the girl as a shield against Frank. But there wasn't time.

Frank put two bullets into her brain. Blood and fluid sprayed everywhere, like a geyser.

chapter
forty

IN THE MORNING, THE ADAMS BROTHERS CAME over to Anna's for breakfast. Frank brought Liz Conway along. Anna had been up most of the night, cleaning.

They sat at the table in strong pure sunlight of the late spring morning, the two daughters dressed up nicely but both quiet and introspective because of all the terrible things that had happened last night.

"So you found the money?" Anna said.

"Yes," David said, "at Myra's, strangely enough. One of her employees, a man named Robinson, had figured out where it was."

Then David told the sad story of young Jane being held prisoner and how Robinson had wanted to help her.

"What'll happen to Jane now?" Anna said.

"We'll find an orphanage for her somewhere," Frank said. "Hopefully there's still time for her to start her life over again."

"And what happens to you two?" Liz said.

David smiled. "Well, my brother heads back to Montana, and I go back to Fort Cree."

Liz said, "Do you think I'll ever hear from your brother again?"

David laughed. "Well, I think you'll hear from him again. And very soon."

"I really want to thank you both," Anna said. She looked exhausted and sad, but there was determination in her blue eyes as she looked down proudly at her daughters. "I guess we can start our lives again, too, can't we, girls?"

They looked at their mother and smiled.

Frank ended up having three helpings of pancakes. The women found this very funny. His brother David just found it very typical.

"I sure can't figure out why you're getting a gut," David said.

Frank smiled and patted his gut. "I sure can't, either, brother. I sure can't either."

Three hours later, after telegraphing ahead for an official of the RCMP to meet Jane, they put the young girl on a train and stood on the platform staring at her as the train pulled out. A great sadness came over the Mountie and the marshal as they thought of all the terrible things that had happened to this little girl.

Then she turned and looked at them and offered a weak little smile. They smiled, too, and then waved.

The mighty engines began to chuff and chug, and the train pulled out of the depot.

"I sure hope she'll be all right," Frank said.

"Me, too, brother," David said. "Me, too."

Then they walked back toward town. As always for men of the law, there was much yet to do.

The Horsemen

by Gary McCarthy

The Ballous were the finest horsemen in the South, a Tennessee family famous for the training and breeding of glorious Thoroughbreds. When the Civil War devastated their home and their lives, they headed West—into the heart of Indian territory. As horsemen, they triumphed. As a family, they endured. But as pioneers in a new land, they faced unimaginable hardship, danger, and ruthless enemies. . . .

Turn the page for a preview of this exciting new western series . . .

The Horsemen

Now available from Diamond Books

November 24, 1863—Just east of Chattanooga, Tennessee

THE CHESTNUT STALLION'S HEAD SNAPPED UP very suddenly. Its nostrils quivered, then flared, testing the wind, tasting the approach of unseen danger. Old Justin Ballou's watchful eye caught the stallion's motion and he also froze, senses focused. For several long moments, man and stallion remained motionless, and then Justin Ballou opened the gate to the paddock and limped toward the tall Thoroughbred. He reached up and his huge, blue-veined hand stroked the stallion's muzzle. "What is it, High Man?" he asked softly. "What now, my friend?"

In answer, the chestnut dipped its head several times and stamped its feet with increasing nervousness. Justin began to speak soothingly to the stallion, his deep, resonant voice flowing like a mystical incantation. Almost at once, the stallion grew calm. After a few minutes, Justin said, as if to an old and very dear friend, "Is it one of General Grant's Union patrols this time, High Man? Have they come to take what little I have left? If so, I will gladly fight them to the death."

The stallion shook its head, rolled its eyes, and snorted as if it could smell Yankee blood. Justin's thick fingers scratched a special place behind the stallion's ear. The chestnut lowered its head to nuzzle the man's chest.

"Don't worry. It's probably another Confederate patrol," Justin said thoughtfully. "But what can they want this time? I have already given them three fine sons and most of your offspring. There is so little left to give—but they know that! Surely they can see my empty stalls and paddocks."

Justin turned toward the road leading past his neat, whitewashed fences that sectioned and cross-sectioned his famous Tennessee horse ranch, known throughout the South as Wildwood Farm. The paddocks were empty and silent. This cold autumn day, there were proud mares with their colts, and prancing fillies blessed the old man's vision or gave him the joy he'd known for so many years. It was the war—this damned killing Civil War. "No more!" Justin cried. "You'll have no more of my fine horses or sons!"

The stallion spun and galloped away. High Man was seventeen years old, long past his prime, but he and a few other Ballou-bred stallions still sired the fastest and handsomest horses in the South. Just watching the chestnut run made Justin feel a little better. High Man was a living testimony to the extraordinarily fine care he'd received all these years at Wildwood Farm. No one would believe that at his ripe age he could still run and kick his heels up like a three-year-old colt.

The stallion ran with such fluid grace that he seemed to float across the earth. When the Thoroughbred reached the far end of the paddock, it skidded to a sliding stop, chest banging hard against the fence. It spun around, snorted, and shook its head for an expected shout of approval.

But not this day. Instead, Justin made himself leave the paddock, chin up, stride halting but resolute. He could hear thunder growing louder. Could it be the sound of cannon from as far away as the heights that General Bragg and his

Rebel army now held in wait of the Union army's expected assault? No, the distance was too great even to carry the roar of heavy artillery. That told Justin that his initial hunch was correct and the sound growing in his ears had to be racing hoofbeats.

But were they enemy or friend? Blue coat or gray? Justin planted his big work boots solidly in the dust of the country road; either way, he would meet them.

"Father!"

He recognized his fourteen-year-old daughter's voice and ignored it, wanting Dixie to stay inside their mansion. Justin drew a pepperbox pistol from his waistband. If this actually was a dreaded Union cavalry patrol, then someone was going to die this afternoon. A man could only be pushed so far and then he had to fight.

"Father!" Dixie's voice was louder now, more strident. "Father!"

Justin reluctantly twisted about to see his daughter and her oldest brother, Houston, running toward him. Both had guns clenched in their fists.

"Who is it!" Houston gasped, reaching Justin first and trying to catch his wind.

Justin did not dignify the stupid question with an answer. In a very few minutes, they would know. "Dixie, go back to the house."

"Please, I . . . I just can't!"

"Dixie! Do as Father says," Houston stormed. "This is no time for arguing. Go to the house!"

Dixie's black eyes sparked. She stood her ground. Houston was twenty-one and a man full grown, but he was still just her big brother. "I'm staying."

Houston's face darkened with anger and his knuckles whitened as he clutched the gun in his fist. "Dammit, you heard . . ."

"Quiet, the both of you!" Justin commanded. "Here they come."

A moment later a dust-shrouded patrol lifted from the earth to come galloping up the road.

"It's *our* boys," Dixie yelped with relief. "It's a Reb patrol!"

"Yeah," Houston said, taking an involuntary step forward, "but they been shot up all to hell!"

Justin slipped his gun back into his waistband and was seized by a flash of dizziness. Dixie moved close, steadying him until the spell passed a moment later. "You all right?"

Justin nodded. He did not know what was causing the dizziness, but the spells seemed to come often these days. No doubt, it was the war. This damned war that the South was steadily losing. And the death of two of his five strapping sons and . . .

Houston had stepped out in front and now he turned to shout, "Mason is riding with them!"

Justin's legs became solid and strong again. Mason was the middle son, the short, serious one that wanted to go into medicine and who read volumes of poetry despite the teasing from his brothers.

Dixie slipped her gun into the pocket of the loose-fitting pants she insisted on wearing around the horses. She glanced up at her father and said, "Mason will be hungry and so will the others. They'll need food and bandaging."

"They'll have both," Justin declared without hesitation, "but no more of my Thoroughbreds!"

"No more," Dixie vowed. "Mason will understand."

"Yeah," Houston said, coming back to stand by his father, "but the trouble is, he isn't in charge. That's a captain he's riding alongside."

Justin was about to speak, but from the corner of his eyes, saw a movement. He twisted, hand instinctively lifting the pepperbox because these woods were crawling with both Union and Confederate deserters, men often half-crazy with fear and hunger.

"Pa, don't you dare shoot me!" Rufus "Ruff" Ballou called, trying to force a smile as he moved forward, long and loose limbed with his rifle swinging at his side.

"Ruff, what the hell you doing hiding in those trees!" Houston demanded, for he too had been startled enough to raise his gun.

If Ruff noticed the heat in his older brother's voice, he chose to ignore it.

"Hell, Houston, I was just hanging back a little to make sure these were friendly visitors."

"It's Mason," Justin said, turning back to the patrol. "And from the looks of these boys, things are going from bad to worse."

There were just six men in the patrol, two officers and four enlisted. One of the enlisted was bent over nearly double with pain, a blossom of red spreading across his left shoulder. Two others were riding double on a runty sorrel.

"That sorrel is gonna drop if it don't get feed and rest," Ruff observed, his voice hardening with disapproval.

"All of their mounts look like they've been chased to hell and back without being fed or watered," Justin stated. "We'll make sure they're watered and grained before these boys leave."

The Ballous nodded. It never occurred to any of them that a horse should ever leave their farm in worse shape than when it had arrived. The welfare of livestock just naturally came first—even over their own physical needs.

Justin stepped forward and raised his hand in greeting. Deciding that none of the horses were in desperate circumstances, he fixed his attention on Mason. He was shocked. Mason was a big man, like his father and brothers, but now he appeared withered—all ridges and angles. His cap was missing and his black hair was wild and unkempt. His cheeks were hollow, and the sleeve of his right arm had been cut away, and now his arm was wrapped in a dirty bandage. The loose, sloppy way he sat his horse told Justin more eloquently than words how weak and weary Mason had become after just eight months of fighting the armies of the North.

The patrol slowed to a trot, then a walk, and Justin saw the captain turn to speak to Mason. Justin couldn't hear the words, but he could see by the senior officer's expression that the man was angry and upset. Mason rode trancelike, eyes fixed on his family, lips a thin, hard slash instead of the expected smile of greeting.

Mason drew his horse to a standstill before his father and brothers. Up close, his appearance was even more shocking.

"Mason?" Justin whispered when his son said nothing. "Mason, are you all right?"

Mason blinked. Shook himself. "Father. Houston. Ruff. Dixie. You're all looking well. How are the horses?"

"What we got left are fine," Justin said cautiously. "Only a few on the place even fit to run. Sold all the fillies and colts last fall. But you knew that."

"You did the right thing to keep Houston and Ruff out of this," Mason said.

Houston and Ruff took a sudden interest in the dirt under their feet. The two youngest Ballou brothers had desperately wanted to join the Confederate army, but Justin had demanded that they remain at Wildwood Farm, where they could help carry on the family business of raising Thoroughbreds. Only now, instead of racetracks and cheering bettors, the Ballou horses swiftly carried messages between the generals of the Confederate armies. Many times the delivery of a vital message depended on horses with pure blazing speed.

"Lieutenant," the captain said, clearing his throat loudly, "I think this chatter has gone on quite long enough. Introduce me."

Mason flushed with humiliation. "Father, allow me to introduce Captain Denton."

Justin had already sized up the captain, and what he saw did not please him. Denton was a lean, straight-backed man. He rode as if he had a rod up his ass and he looked like a mannequin glued to the saddle. He was an insult to the fine tradition of Southern cavalry officers.

"Captain," Justin said without warmth, "if you'll order your patrol to dismount, we'll take care of your wounded and these horses."

"Private Wilson can't ride any farther," Denton said. "And there isn't time for rest."

"But you *have* to," Justin argued. "These horses are—"

"Finished," Denton said. "We must have replacements, that's why we are here, Mr. Ballou."

Justin paled ever so slightly. "Hate to tell you this, Captain, but I'm afraid you're going to be disappointed. I've already given all the horses I can to the Confederacy—sons, too."

Denton wasn't listening. His eyes swept across the paddock.

"What about *that* one," he said, pointing toward High Man. "He looks to be in fine condition."

"He's past his racing prime," Houston argued. "He's our foundation sire now and is used strictly for breeding."

"Strictly for breeding?" Denton said cryptically. "Mr. Ballou, there is not a male creature on this earth who would not like to—"

"Watch your tongue, sir!" Justin stormed. "My daughter's honor will not be compromised!"

Captain Denton's eyes jerked sideways to Dixie and he blushed. Obviously, he had not realized Dixie was a girl with her baggy pants and a felt slouch hat pulled down close to her eyebrows. And a Navy Colt hanging from her fist.

"My sincere apologies." The captain dismissed her and his eyes came to rest on the barns. "You've got horses in those stalls?"

"Yes, but—"

"I'd like to see them," Denton said, spurring his own flagging mount forward.

Ruff grabbed his bit. "Hold up there, Captain, you haven't been invited."

"And since when does an officer of the Confederacy need to beg permission for horses so that *your* countrymen, as well as mine, can live according to our own laws!"

"*I'm* the law on this place," Justin thundered. "And my mares are in foal. They're not going to war, Captain. Neither they nor the last of my stallions are going to be chopped to pieces on some battlefield or have their legs ruined while trying to pull supply wagons. These are *Thoroughbred* horses, sir! Horses bred to race."

"The race," Denton said through clenched teeth, "is to see if we can bring relief to our men who are, this very moment, fighting and dying at Lookout Mountain and Missionary Ridge."

Denton's voice shook with passion. "The plundering armies of General Ulysses Grant, General George Thomas, and his Army of the Cumberland are attacking our soldiers right now, and God help me if I've ever seen such slaughter! Our boys are dying, Mr. Ballou! Dying for the right to determine the South's great destiny. We—not you and your piddling horses—are making the ultimate sacrifices! But maybe your attitude has a lot to do with why you married a Cherokee Indian woman."

Something snapped behind Justin Ballou's obsidian eyes. He saw the faces of his two oldest sons, one reported to have been blown to pieces by a Union battery in the battle of Bull Run and the other trampled to death in a bloody charge at Shiloh. Their proud mother's Cherokee blood had made them the first in battle and the first in death.

Justin lunged, liver-spotted hands reaching upward. Too late Captain Denton saw murder in the old man's eyes. He tried to rein his horse off, but Justin's fingers clamped on his coat and his belt. With a tremendous heave, Denton was torn from his saddle and hurled to the ground. Justin growled like a huge dog as his fingers crushed the breath out of Denton's life.

He would have broken the Confederate captain's neck if his sons had not broken his stranglehold. Two of the mounted soldiers reached for their pistols, but Ruff's own rifle made them freeze and then slowly raise their hands.

"Pa!" Mason shouted, pulling Justin off the nearly unconscious officer. "Pa, stop it!"

As suddenly as it had flared, Justin's anger ended, and he had to be helped to his feet. He glared down at the wheezing cavalry officer and his voice trembled when he said, "Captain Denton, I don't know how the hell you managed to get a commission in Jeff Davis's army, but I do know this: lecture me about sacrifice for the South again and I will break your fool neck! Do you hear me!"

The captain's eyes mirrored raw animal fear. "Lieutenant Ballou," he choked at Mason, "I *order* you in the name of the Army of the Confederacy to confiscate fresh horses!"

"Go to hell."

"I'll have you court-martialed and shot for insubordination!"

Houston drew his pistol and aimed it at Denton's forehead. "Maybe you'd better change your tune, Captain."

"No!"

Justin surprised them all by coming to Denton's defense. "If you shoot him—no matter how much he deserves to be shot—our family will be judged traitors."

"But . . ."

"Put the gun away," Justin ordered wearily. "I'll give him fresh horses."

"Pa!" Ruff cried. "What are you going to give to him? Our mares?"

"Yes, but not all of them. Just the youngest and the strongest. And those matched three-year-old stallions you and Houston are training."

"But, Pa," Ruff protested, "they're just green broke."

"I know, but this will season them in a hurry," Justin said levelly. "Besides, there's no choice. High Man leaves Wildwood Farm over my dead body."

"Yes, sir," Ruff said, knowing his father was not running a bluff.

Dixie turned away in anger and started toward the house. "I'll see we get food cooking for the soldiers and some fresh bandages for Private Wilson."

A moment later, Ruff stepped over beside the wounded soldier. "Here, let me give you a hand down. We'll go up to the house and take a look at that shoulder."

Wilson tried to show his appreciation as both Ruff and Houston helped him to dismount. "Much obliged," he whispered. "Sorry to be of trouble."

Mason looked to his father. "Sir, I'll take responsibility for your horses."

"How can you do that?" Houston demanded of his brother. "These three-year-old stallions and our mares will go crazy amid all that cannon and rifle fire. No one but us can control them. It would be—"

"Then you and Ruff need to come on back with us," Mason said.

"No!" Justin raged. "I paid for their replacements! I've got the papers saying that they can't be drafted or taken into the Confederate army."

"Maybe not," Mason said, "but they can volunteer to help us save lives up on the mountains where General Bragg is in danger of being overrun, and where our boys are dying for lack of medical attention."

"No!" Justin choked. "I've given too much already!"

"Pa, we won't fight. We'll just go to handle the horses." Ruff placed his hand on his father's shoulder. "No fighting," he pledged, looking past his father at the road leading toward Chattanooga and the battlefields. "I swear it."

Justin shook his head, not believing a word of it. His eyes shifted from Mason to Houston and finally settled on Ruff. "You boys are *fighters*! Oh, I expect you'll even try to do as you promised, but you won't be able to once you smell gunpowder and death. You'll fight and get yourselves killed, just like Micha and John."

Mason shook his head vigorously. "Pa, I swear that once the horses are delivered and hitched to those ambulances and supply wagons, I'll send Houston and Ruff back to you. All right?"

After a long moment, Justin finally managed to nod his head. "Come along," he said to no one in particular, "we'll get our Thoroughbreds ready."

But Captain Denton's thin lips twisted in anger. "I want a *dozen* horses! Not one less will do. And I still want that big chestnut stallion in that paddock for my personal mount."

Houston scoffed with derision, "Captain, I've seen some fools in my short lifetime, but none as big as you."

"At least," Denton choked, "my daddy didn't buy my way out of the fighting."

Houston's face twisted with fury and his hand went for the Army Colt strapped to his hip. It was all that Ruff could do to keep his older brother from gunning down the ignorant cavalry officer.

"You *are* a fool," Ruff gritted at the captain when he'd calmed Houston down. "And if you should be lucky enough to survive this war, you'd better pray that you never come across me or any of my family."

Denton wanted to say something. His mouth worked but Ruff's eyes told him he wouldn't live long enough to finish even a single sentence, so the captain just clamped his mouth shut and spun away in a trembling rage.